Good Time Charlie

Good Time Charlie

By
Donnie Prince

This book is a work of fiction. References to real people, events, establishments, organizations or locales are intended only to provide a sense of authenticity, and are used fictitiously. All other characters, and all incidents and dialogue, are drawn from the author's imagination and are not to be construed as real.

Cover designed by Kevin Williamson.

ISBN: 979-8-218-07348-0

1

"Welcome back ladies and gentlemen. For those of you who are just joining us, this is Bill Thomas and Greg Wilson with WCGN Radio, coming to you from historic Belmont Park. We are entering the bottom of the ninth inning of tonight's ballgame where last place Chicago is trailing 4-1, to division leading St. Louis. Tonight, is the last game of the regular season, another in a series of lackluster performances by Chicago who is in danger of losing the fourth game of a four-game series.

"Tonight's ballgame has been a microcosm of what has become a second half collapse for Chicago. The Chicago nine has completely fallen apart since the all-star break."

"That's exactly right Bill. Chicago, who were three games over .500 at the all-star break, have fallen to pieces in the second half. Highlighted by consecutive game losing streaks of eight and eleven games since July. The only bright spots for Chicago in the second half of the season has been the hitting and defense of All Star center fielder Jose Francone, who will be eligible for free agency at the end of the year, and the pitching of hard throwing third year starting pitcher Charlie Pace."

"Once again, this season, Greg, as the Chicago ball club has faded out of playoff contention in the second half of the season, management has traded away some of the key components of the roster. Since those players, starting pitcher John Trotter, and short stop Jose Cordero in particular, have left for greener pastures, this team has been unable to get any sort of chemistry going on the field. And

1

in large part as a result of those trades the team has come unraveled over the last eight weeks of the season.

"Leading off the inning for Chicago and pinch hitting in the pitcher's spot will be reserve infielder Scott Hamilton. Hamilton hitting just .193 on the year with two homeruns and 21 RBI's. Hamilton takes a pitch outside, the count, 1 ball and no strikes."

"Bill, what do you think it will take for Chicago to turn their fortunes around and get this ball club back to playing competitive baseball again next season?"

"Greg, it seems to me, as we see Hamilton take ball two, that the Chicago organization has got to make a commitment to playing an entire 162 game season with the emphasis on winning ball games now. The organization cannot keep trading away the nucleus of the team once they get behind in the second half of the season the way we have this year. We must try to build a culture of winning in the clubhouse.

"This ball club has got to build some depth in their farm system. Build unity in the locker room and develop the attitude that they are in it to win it, if they are going to compete with teams like St Louis and Los Angeles. And right now, I am sad to say the organization is not doing that; as Hamilton swings and pops the ball up in foul territory down the first base line. St Louis first baseman Steve Grace moves under it and makes the play, one down."

"Jaquan Jones will be the next batter up for Chicago. Jones playing third base and batting a respectable .267 with 12 home runs and 56 RBI's.

"You are exactly right Bill, as Jones swings and misses at strike one. I realize we are in the era of roster turnover with free agency. The teams like St. Louis, and Cincinnati who seem to make the fewest changes to their rosters and develop talent throughout their minor league farm system, go on to contend year after year by keeping their younger players on the rosters. Whether they are in the playoff hunt or not, and that philosophy wins ball games; as Jones takes ball two outside."

"Those teams like Boston, Atlanta, and the Knights, along with St. Louis and San Francisco are in the playoff hunt every year because they make winning championships the priority; as Jones hits a sharp line drive right at left fielder Randy Roberts, who makes the catch for out number two."

"The next batter for Chicago, due up with two outs here in the bottom of the ninth inning is right fielder Tony Page. Page hitting just .203 on the season, and Chicago down to their last out trailing 4-1, in what has been a long season for the home standing Chicago team. Page swings at the first pitch and hits a lazy fly ball to left center field. The left fielder Roberto Sorento is under it and makes the play. St. Louis wins the ball game and is on to the playoffs for the fifth consecutive season as Division Champions."

"Well Bill, with the loss tonight, the Chicago team has concluded another disappointing losing season. And the question everyone in Chicago and around baseball must be asking is what will it take for this organization to get back into contention again?"

"With tonight's loss, their seventh loss in their last eight games, the team finishes the regular season with 73 wins and 89 losses.

"And with the season now over, the Chicago faithful also must be somewhat concerned about the health of their star pitcher Charlie Pace. The team's former first round draft pick who in his third full season in the major leagues has 21 of the teams 73 wins against just 7 losses, while compiling a league leading ERA of 2.12. Pace also leads the league in strike outs with 302 and would appear to be a shoe in to win this year's award as the most outstanding pitcher in professional baseball, despite missing his last three starts due to soreness in his right elbow. Pace is rumored to be facing elbow surgery in the next few days."

2

Ten Years Later

In a lobby overlooking the left field bleachers, off the west wing of Belmont Park, the home offices for the Chicago baseball team, sits an attractive young woman. The heel of her right high heel shoe taps impatiently beneath her. She smiles nervously, looking toward the lady sitting behind the receptionist desk.

"Nervous Loraine?" the lady asked.

"Yes," the young woman replied.

"Let me go in there and see how long he will be."

The receptionist soon came back out into the lobby, "Mr. Volkmann will see you now. Good luck Loraine."

"Thank you," the young woman replied. She stood up and straightened her dress. Then she walked confidently into the office.

"Come in Loraine, have a seat," Mr. Volkmann said, as he motioned for Loraine to take a seat in a chair across from him. "Loraine, can I get you anything to drink, coffee, a glass of water perhaps?"

"No thank you, Mr. Volkmann."

"Loraine, as you are aware we have a position that will be coming available within the National Merchandising Division, of the Licensed Products Sales Team. We are considering you as a candidate to fill the position. The role of Sales Manager of our Chicago Licensed logo products. If you were offered the position, there would be a substantial increase in responsibility and along with it a pay increase and bonus opportunities.

5

"In this position you would be managing a team of 24 people, including ten outside sales reps, ten inside sales employees, and four clerical office staff. Is that something you would be interested in if the position were offered to you?"

"Yes sir, I would."

"You have done an excellent job since joining the organization Loraine, and we believe you have a bright future here."

"Thank you, Mr. Volkmann," Loraine replied.

"Before the final decision is made, we want to send you to our minor league farm team in Myrtle Beach, South Carolina for the summer season. There you will have an opportunity to work as the General Manager for the Myrtle Beach Seahawks, our Double AA minor league team in Myrtle Beach. This will give you an opportunity to manage a group of 30 staff people who are a part of the organization there. You will have complete managerial control over all the advertising, beverage, food and promotional product sales, maintenance of the facilities and ticket sales and promotions for the upcoming season. Everyone at the facility will report to you, except of course for the coaching staff and the players, trainers, equipment managers, etc.

"This will give you an opportunity to run the show down there. And give us an opportunity to evaluate you for this sales management position which will be coming available at year's end.

"This would require you to move to Myrtle Beach for the summer. If you choose to pursue this Sales Manager opportunity, we will provide you with a furnished condominium for the summer at no expense to you. Is this something you would like to do?"

"Yes sir, thank you sir," Loraine replied.

"There is one special project I would like to put you in charge of this summer while you are in Myrtle Beach working with the Seahawks. Loraine what do you know about Charlie Pace?"

"I know that Charlie Pace was a former player here in Chicago ten years or so ago, sir. I know he won the Most Outstanding Player Award in professional baseball one year while playing here in Chicago. And we still sell quite a few of his jerseys in the sports memorabilia store here at the ballpark."

"Charlie Pace was the team's first round selection when he was in high school," Mr. Volkmann said. "He was the first overall pick of the professional baseball draft that summer. Charlie then pitched in the team's minor league system for three years before making the big-league roster here in Chicago. Charlie pitched for the team three years here in Chicago. He made the All-Star team twice during those three years. Charlie was a fan favorite while he was in Chicago. Charlie had the best fastball in the major leagues during those three years. His jersey sales during those years were among the top selling jerseys in all professional sports.

"During his third season here in Chicago, Charlie began to develop elbow problems. After the season he underwent Tommy John surgery on his right elbow. After the surgery Charlie developed a staph infection in his elbow, and for the next two years he could not pitch at all. Once his arm healed, the velocity on his fastball never completely returned. He was not the same pitcher. For the past seven seasons Charlie has been a player/coach with the Myrtle Beach Seahawks. Charlie has pitched well during his years in Myrtle Beach, but the loss of velocity on his fastball has kept him from ever being able to return to the top of the game as a player. At times he has shown the ability to pitch at the major league level again, but not consistently. His story is somewhat of a mystery.

"Over the years since Charlie's surgery there has been a lot of interest here in Chicago and around professional baseball circles in Charlie's story. Loraine I am sure you have seen some of the sports documentary series programs on the Sports Channel."

"Yes sir, I have."

"The organization has been approached by the network about doing a documentary on Charlie Pace. We believe the series on Charlie would be a great PR piece for the organization and would give us a chance to honor Charlie here at the ballpark at the end of the season, on the 10-year anniversary of Charlie winning the Most Outstanding Player Award.

"While you are in Myrtle Beach, we would like for you to work closely with Charlie on the documentary piece. We would like for you to represent the organization as our liaison with the Sports Channel production crew, Charlie and the Seahawks during the season. Then we would want you and Charlie to come back to Chicago at the end of the year so we can recognize Charlie during our final home series with St Louis at the end of the season."

"That sounds exciting, sir. It sounds like a wonderful opportunity. I will do my best to make that happen, sir."

"Alright then, it's settled. See Mrs. Stone on your way out and she will help you make your travel arrangements. Best of luck to you Loraine this summer in Myrtle Beach."

3

The sun was just coming up over the horizon. Sunlight turning the sky from black to deep purple. As the orange sun burst over top of the houses lining the sound shoreline along Murrells Inlet, a man and his dog make their way out the front door of a sound front condominium, then down a row of steps. Walking briskly, they turn right across a wooden plank pier, leading to a row of kayaks spread out alongside the riverbank.

The handsome young man in his mid-thirties now, stretched his hands out above his head. Yawning as he shakes off the morning fog, he looks down at the black lab standing next to him. Bending forward now with his hands on his hips, he rotates his body in a counterclockwise motion stretching out the muscles in his legs and lower back. Then spreading his legs out wide he leans forward bending over at the waist twisting his torso from side to side. Soon after he leans backwards and around again, loosening the muscles in his upper arms and shoulders. Then clasping his hands together arms stretched out behind him, he leans forward again loosening his powerful wrist and finally his elbows.

Within a few minutes he was lowering a kayak in the water. And with the black lab taking his position in the front seat of the kayak, Charlie entered the boat and began to paddle out into the inlet. Quickly moving out beyond the mouth of the inlet, the boat passed the shoreline and into the Atlantic Ocean. It was nearly 7 am by this time. For the next half hour, he briskly paddled the kayak farther out into the ocean. Then turning right, now moving south, parallel to the beach about 100 yards offshore, he reached his cruising speed. The kayak splitting through the water, sweat now pouring off his powerful tan shoulders. The ocean on this early morning was slick as glass, as they made their way down the shoreline. Charlie and Bubba looking occasionally back to their right at the rows of hotels and oceanfront homes, their silhouette frames now illuminated by the early morning sunlight, perched atop the dunes beneath them.

It was a little after 8 by the time Charlie pulled the kayak onshore, about 50 yards from the Apache Pier. He slipped a pair of running shoes out of the boat's watertight compartment. Once the shoe laces were tied, he and his dog began to run wind sprints back and forth for the next hour along the beach. After the running was complete, the two walked the 100 yards or so up the shoreline across the sand dunes, and entered the convenient store located at the top of the hill next to the pier.

"You guys are running a little late this morning, aren't you Charlie," said the older man working behind the counter.

"Yeah, Bubba overslept this morning, didn't you boy," Charlie replied as he leaned forward and rubbed the dog's head. "I need to get me some orange juice and a banana, Mr. Jones. And Bubba needs him a sausage biscuit don't you boy," Charlie continued as he walked briskly between the isles, then reaching into the beverage freezer for a bottle of juice.

"Better yet, how about you fix a sausage biscuit for Bubba and one for me too, Mr. Jones."

"Sure thing, Charlie. I tell you what, I am excited about the start of the baseball season this year. Is Juan Romero going to be back with the team again this year or is he moving up to Triple AAA?"

"Romero will be back here with the Seahawks to start the season but if he continues to pitch the way he did the end of last year I suspect he will finish the season in Chicago with the big team," answered Charlie. "Romero was rated as the top minor league pitcher in the Chicago organization at the end of last year."

"That Romero sure is a handsome kid. Last year when he would bring the frozen lemonade to the cart girls selling lemonade to the tourist on the beach near the pier, the girls flocked all over him. He looks like he stepped off the cover of a fashion magazine. The girls went crazy over that boy last summer. I bet he draws a bunch of female fans to the ballpark, doesn't he Charlie?"

"Yeah, he does. You know we call Romero, 'Romeo' in the dugout. That boy has got the girls swarming around him everywhere he goes when we are around town, and when we're on the road too. When he worked for the beverage company making deliveries last summer, he drove those college girls working in the lemonade stands nuts. We would have cart girls calling the office for Romeo to bring them lemonade even when they didn't need any more just so they could talk to him. It got so bad near the end of the summer that we had to take him off making deliveries to the cart girls, and just send him into grocery stores. Romeo will never have trouble finding a date, that's for sure."

"Must be a nice problem to have. At my age I can only dream about those kinds of problems," Mr. Jones laughingly said.

"Charlie, I was reading in the paper the other day that you all are going to have a new General Manager this season. A woman, the paper said, Loraine Feltzer. There was a picture of this Feltzer girl in the paper. She was a real looker, Charlie. Have you met her? Did you know her when you were in Chicago?"

"No Mr. Jones, I've never met Ms. Feltzer. The players normally don't have much interaction with management. We pretty much stick to playing baseball and they run the operation side of things. I probably won't be spending a lot of time with this new GM."

"Well, she sure was a looker Charlie, looks to be a real pretty girl. If you do get a chance to meet her, put in a good word for me, will you?" Mr. Jones chuckled.

"Yeah, sure Mr. Jones. Whenever I do see her, I will let her know you're interested in her just in case she's looking for a boyfriend while she's in town this summer."

"You do that Charlie."

4

"Good morning, everyone," Loraine said standing at the podium in the conference room of the Seahawk's office for the first time.

"I appreciate you all being here to meet me this morning. I am looking forward to getting to work with all of you this summer. I am excited to be here, and I have heard nothing but wonderful things about Myrtle Beach and the Seahawks. I am looking forward to spending the summer with you all. I know if we work together, we will have a great season. I really don't have a lot of news to tell you this morning, other than to introduce myself.

"I have been working in Chicago with the baseball organization for seven years now. My background before joining the organization was in the fashion industry. Since I have been with the organization I have been in merchandising, working mainly in the licensed product sales division, mostly with inside sales. This is my first opportunity to be involved with the baseball side of operations. This is also my first time working on a project outside of Chicago. So, I will be relying heavily on your expertise in ticket sales, game promotions and selling stadium advertising this summer. I look forward to learning more about those aspects of the organization and how you do things here in Myrtle Beach.

"You had a great season in attendance and merchandise sales performance last year, so I do not intend to change a thing this year. We just want to continue to build on the momentum from last year. I am sure that we will have just as successful a season as we have these past few years leading the Coastal Beach league in attendance.

"Well, that's enough about me. We have all summer to get acquainted. Thank you again for being here this morning. Now let's take some time to enjoy this nice breakfast and get to know each other a bit."

Once her impromptu speech was over, Loraine and the others made their way through the breakfast buffet line and then mingled in the conference room, as Loraine met her staff and co-workers for the first time. After the meeting was over, Loraine and her Assistant General Manager, Doris Thomas, sat down and had a visit in Loraine's new office.

Doris was an attractive woman in her late forties. She had grown up in the Myrtle Beach area. Happily married for the past 25 years, she and her husband Fred had two teenage daughters. Doris had been with the Seahawks for the past fourteen seasons. She had started in ticket sales and over the years worked in advertising, scheduling, accounting and on field promotions. She had been responsible for the facility rental and also had some experience with stadium maintenance. Before leaving Chicago, Mr. Volkmann told Loraine, Doris would be her go to person for anything she needed to know about the Seahawks and Myrtle Beach.

"Well Doris," Loraine said as she sat down and took a seat behind her new desk for the first time, "they told me in Chicago that you are the best Assistant GM in the Chicago minor league system, hands down."

"Thank you, Ms. Feltzer."

"Please, call me Loraine."

"Alright then, thank you, Loraine."

"Tell me a little about Myrtle Beach, Doris. I understand you have been here most of your life."

"I love Myrtle Beach. It is a small town most of the year, a great place to raise a family. Then in the spring and summer the beach, golf courses, shopping, and restaurants fill up with tourists. Once April gets here, Myrtle Beach becomes a major city on the weekends. Later when school gets out and the tourists come for the summer, Myrtle Beach is also an entertainment destination. It's one of the top five in the United States. It is quiet and peaceful part of the year, and touristy and exciting in the summer. It is a great place to live because of the variety of the seasons, the mild climate, and the beaches. I think you will really enjoy it here this summer."

"During our meeting earlier today, Doris, I said there were not going to be any major changes this season. I would like for you and I to work closely together to keep the systems you all have in place now so we can keep things going as usual."

"That's fine Loraine. I will be happy to help you any way I can."

"There is one other thing Doris that I didn't mention in our meeting that I would like you to help me with this summer."

"Sure, what's that Loraine?"

"The Sports Network has approached the baseball organization in Chicago about doing a documentary series on Charlie Pace. Part of my being sent here this summer was to work with the network on the project and coordinate with the organization's front office to get the documentary filmed. Tell me Doris, what do you know about Charlie Pace?"

"Charlie Pace is great guy. And in addition to that, he is about the most gorgeous thing you will ever lay your eyes on! Sorry, but that is just a fact. Everybody around here calls him 'Good Time Charlie.' He first came down here after his elbow surgery. For a couple of seasons, he just worked out and tried to rehabilitate his arm. But for whatever reason, he never made it back to the big leagues.

"Charlie is a real celebrity here in Myrtle Beach. I guess there aren't a lot of former Most Outstanding Player Award winners playing minor league baseball. He is treated like royalty everywhere he goes. He lives here year-round now. And every time I see him, he has a pretty girl on his arm. But it is never the same girl twice.

"I know Charlie was married to a weather girl at one of the television stations back when he was playing with the team in Chicago. The story is, that once Charlie injured his elbow and the surgery and recovery didn't go well, the weather girl left Charlie for a hockey player. And since then, Charlie is real non-committal toward women. He still likes women; he just likes to be dating more than one at the time from what I understand.

"Charlie lives by himself down at the North Myrtle Beach Marina. He's sort of quiet until you get to know him. He spends a lot of time with a lawyer friend of his, Steve Wilson, who happens to be the controlling partner of one of our largest advertisers."

"Which company," Loraine asked.

"Bubba's Frozen Lemonade."

"I'm familiar with them, they sell their lemonade and frozen drink mixers at Belmont Park in Chicago. Is their home office here in Myrtle Beach?"

"Yes, they have a huge business. They sell their lemonade in all the area grocery stores and in some major food retailers across the South Eastern United States as well. They sell some of their product as drink mixers now to many of the restaurants and nightclubs in Myrtle Beach and most of the golf courses. I understand they have over 100 lemonade stands just in the Myrtle Beach area alone. Selling on the beaches, at hotels, the golf courses, they are big time.

They are our major advertiser here at the ball park. They also sponsor a youth program, 'Bubba Ball', where they organize youth baseball camps for disadvantaged and handicap children. You will see a lot of Steve and Charlie together here at the ball park and around town."

"Doris, if you would, please get in touch with Charlie Pace and set up a meeting so I can meet him and discuss this documentary. I want to get started on this as soon as possible."

"Will do, Loraine."

5

It was a little before 10 when Charlie pulled his Jeep into the Seahawks Stadium parking lot. It was a warm breezy day for mid-March, just five weeks before the Seahawks home opener. Charlie exited the Jeep wearing a t-shirt, ball cap, pair of blue jeans and flip flops. Quickly making his way through the stadium gates, and upstairs to the General Manager's office for his 10 am meeting with Loraine.

"Hey there Doris, how's it going," Charlie asked as he walked over toward Doris' desk, sitting just outside the door of Loraine's office. "So how you like your new boss from the big city?"

"She's a nice girl, Charlie. I think she is going to be good for us this summer."

"What about after this summer Doris? You make it sound like she isn't going to be here long."

"That's right, she is here just for the summer," Doris replied. "She told us that when she first got here. Sounds like she is on the fast track to some big job back in Chicago. She is going to be here in Myrtle Beach just for the summer, and then she is headed back to Chicago for good if all goes well."

"I see, so what does she want to see me about Doris?"

"You're going to have to ask her that. She's on the phone right now so just sit down over there a minute," Doris said as she directed Charlie to a seat out in the lobby, "and I'll go on in and tell her you are here."

Charlie took a seat and after a few minutes Doris walked back out into the lobby to get him, "Loraine's off the phone Charlie. She'll see you now."

19

Charlie got up and walked across the lobby to Loraine's office where Loraine was sitting behind her desk. Once Charlie walked in, Loraine stood up and walked around the desk and extended her right hand to greet him. Loraine was wearing a tightly fitted white dress that accentuated her athletic figure, and complimented her shoulder length raven black hair and piercing blue eyes, which were the color of sapphires. Loraine was dressed like she had just stepped off the cover of a fashion magazine. As soon as Charlie laid eyes on Loraine, he was smitten with her.

"Hello Charlie, I'm Loraine Feltzer. It's a pleasure to meet you. I have heard a lot about you."

"Well, it's nice to meet you too, Loraine."

"Have a seat," Loraine continued as she gestured toward one of the two chairs in front of her desk. She then took a seat in the other chair to Charlie's left. For the next few minutes, they exchanged pleasantries, as they got to know each other a bit. It was the kind of conversational foreplay that goes on between two attractive people who are meeting each other for the first time. Loraine could see why Doris had told her in their first meeting that Charlie would be the sexiest man she would ever meet. The rugged good looks, the easy smile, his relaxed demeanor. Charlie was a player. He'd always had a way with the ladies, and Loraine couldn't help but notice.

"It's not every day you get to meet a former Most Outstanding Player award winner," remarked Loraine.

"Thanks Loraine, but that was a long time ago," Charlie replied.

"Not that long ago, ten years to be exact," Loraine said calmly while brushing back her dark black hair behind her right shoulder.

"It seems like another person's life sometimes. But thank you for remembering," Charlie said.

"Well, tell me a little about yourself, Charlie?"

"I'm originally from St Petersburg, Florida. I grew up in St Petersburg and went to high school there. The Chicago ball club drafted me out of high school, and I signed with them right after graduation. I spent three years pitching in the minor leagues before making the roster with the big team. I pitched in Chicago for three years and then I had surgery on my elbow. The surgery went fine, but I developed a staph infection in my arm after the surgery. Once that happened, I never really got over it, and I've been pitching in the minor leagues ever since."

"So, you have been playing baseball with the Seahawks here in Myrtle Beach since the surgery?"

"Yes Loraine, that's right."

"Do you live here year-round?" asked Loraine.

"Yes, I do now."

"You must like it here Charlie, to have stayed in Myrtle Beach playing baseball all this time."

"I love Myrtle Beach. I like the weather. It's a great place to be in the summer time, and the winters are mild here too. I play a lot of golf now, and there are tons of great golf courses in the area. Myrtle Beach is home for me now.

"Enough about me Loraine, tell me a little about you?" Charlie said.

"I'm a native of Chicago. Born and raised there, as you say here in the south. I went to college in New York, majored in fashion merchandising. After graduating from college, I spent four years trying to find work as a model in the fashion industry there. But I got tired of eating salads every day. I was always having to watch my figure, and also because I didn't have any money."

"I'm sure people are still watching your figure, Loraine," Charlie casually replied, while flashing that million dollar smile back in Loraine's direction.

'Wow, he is smooth' Loraine thought to herself. *'I am going to have to watch myself around this guy.'*

"So, after giving modeling a try I moved back to Chicago," Loraine continued, "where I was lucky enough to land a job with the team's merchandising department and I've been there ever since. Now I am here for the summer working with the Seahawks. And after the season I will be going back to Chicago."

"So, Myrtle Beach, and the General Manager's job with the Seahawks, is just a stopover for you this summer?"

"Yes, and you are part of the reason I am here, Charlie."

"Really? How's that Loraine?"

"Charlie, it looks like you and I will be spending a lot of time together this summer!" Loraine said excitedly, as she leaned forward and rested her right hand gently upon Charlie's left knee. "I've got some exciting news to share with you, which is why I wanted to meet with you this morning. The team's front office has been approached by the Sports Channel, about doing a documentary series, one of those hour-long sports documentary segments, on the 10th anniversary of you winning the Most Outstanding Player Award. The Chicago organization is very excited about this opportunity. That is part of the reason for me being here in Myrtle Beach this summer. Mr. Volkmann has sent me here to work with you and the television network as the team's liaison in filming the documentary. Isn't that exciting! And at the end of the season the team would like for you to come back to Chicago and be honored at our final home series, in commemoration of the 10th anniversary of you winning the Most Outstanding Player Award!"

For the next minute or so there was an awkward silence as Charlie just sat there. It was as if he was looking back into some distant painful memory. Loraine was perplexed by the silence. Charlie's facial expression went blank; he didn't say anything.

After a bit Loraine spoke up. "This is a real honor, Charlie. The front office is really excited about this! Everyone in Chicago whom I have spoken to has said that they want this for you. They want you to be able to tell your story in the documentary. The team wants to honor your accomplishments in Chicago at the ballpark in our final home series. This is something to be excited about Charlie!"

"Look Loraine, I appreciate what you are saying, but this isn't for me. This documentary is not something I would be interested in doing."

"I don't understand Charlie?" Loraine asked. She could sense Charlie was upset. She was not sure what to say.

"This is a great opportunity for you to tell your story to the world, Charlie. I can assure you it will be tastefully done. It will be a tribute to you and your accomplishments in professional baseball. It is a great honor and the organization is excited about you coming back to Chicago and recognizing you at the end of the regular season. I wish you would reconsider."

"It is flattering Loraine. And I am very appreciative of the offer, really, I am. But that Charlie Pace, the young guy who pitched in the majors and won the Most Outstanding Player Award, that guy, he and I parted company a long time ago. Those days are behind me. The memory of what I was then and what might have been are something I put behind me a long time ago. I am at peace with the person I am now. I am happy here. I am not interested in doing the documentary."

6

"Well, hello there, Good Timer," Steve Wilson said, as Charlie and Bubba came walking through the warehouse doors. "What did you think of your new GM?"

"Nice girl," Charlie replied.

"Is that it? Nice girl? She looked like a nice, beautiful young woman in that picture of her in the paper. You didn't notice, when you met with her this morning?"

"She is a nice girl, and very attractive," Charlie said casually as he and Bubba made their way over to one of the Bubba's Frozen Lemonade delivery trucks lined across the 30,000 square foot warehouse. "Wow, that is a nice paint job on this truck," Charlie said as he wiped his left hand across the truck body with a picture of a black lab painted on the side.

"Yeah, the art department did a great job with that new logo design," remarked Steve. "And if things go the way I think they will, we will be needing 10 more of these trucks once we sign the account with the Food Chain. We will be shipping Bubba's Frozen Lemonade and Mixers across the country once that deal is finalized. To 300 new grocery stores in 10 states.

"Who would have ever imagined eight years ago when we were selling those frozen lemonade mixers to a few bars and nightclubs that today we would be talking about a company with 35 million dollars in sales?" Steve said. "But here we are. Old Bubba has come a long way."

"Yeah, he has," Charlie replied as he leaned over and rubbed Bubba's ears with both hands. Bubba's tail wagging happily behind him. "You have done a great job managing all of this Steve. Bubba could have never done it without you."

"Thanks Charlie," Steve replied. "So, tell me, was there any other news this morning you want to tell me about after speaking with Loraine?"

Charlie could sense right away from the inflection in Steve's voice that he was asking about something specific, but he let it go on a little anyway.

"No, not really," Charlie replied.

"Nothing? What did the two of you talk about?" Steve asked.

"Oh, she just wanted to meet me. Told me a little about herself, asked some questions about Myrtle Beach. What it was like to live here, things like that."

"I see," Steve continued, "what about the documentary with the Sports Channel? What did she have to say about that?"

"Here we go," Charlie said, "now we are getting down to it. How do you know about that?"

"Doris told me," answered Steve.

"Doris, I should have known she knew. I could tell she knew what the meeting was about when I asked her this morning. If you tell Doris Thomas something you want to keep private, you might as well put it up on a billboard for everyone in Myrtle Beach to know.

"When did she tell you?"

"Two days ago," Steve replied.

"You have known for two days, and you didn't say anything about it?"

"It was a surprise!" Steve said laughingly as he reached over and rubbed Bubba's back. "I told Bubba about it. Didn't he tell you?"

Charlie rolled his eyes in disgust. "No, Bubba didn't tell me. But it doesn't matter. There isn't going to be a documentary."

"What? What's up with that? Doris said it was a sure thing. The Sports Channel was coming into town, and they were going to be in and out of town spending four weeks or so off and on. Following you around this summer filming and doing interviews. Then you were going to be honored the last week of the season in Chicago. Man, I was looking forward to being a part of all that. What happened? I thought that was a done deal?"

"It was a done deal with the network and the baseball organization in Chicago, but not with me," Charlie replied resolutely. "I don't want to do that."

"Why not?" Steve asked.

"I've got my reasons," Charlie said as he gave Steve the distinct impression, he didn't want to talk about it. Steve sensing the change in Charlie's mood and knowing him as a close friend, could tell the topic was off limits.

"Hey Charlie, I'm sorry to hear that. I am sure you have your reasons. You know I have some things in my past too that I would like to keep to myself. We both do. If you want to talk about it let me know. If not, I won't bring the subject up again."

"Steve, man, don't worry about that. I didn't mean to bark at you that way. You know, we have it made here now. I have so much to be thankful for. I love my life here, would not trade it for the world. Just some things in the past, that I would like to leave in the past."

"Me too, brother," Steve said as he put his hand on Charlie's shoulder. "I understand."

7

For the next three weeks, once Charlie and Bubba completed their morning workout, they spent most of their day helping Steve in the Bubba's Frozen Lemonade warehouses. As expected, Steve had closed the deal with the Food Chain which increased the company's business by nearly 40 percent. The new customer relationship with the Food Chain over the next year would increase company sales to nearly $50 million dollars.

The additional sales would also solidify the need for more management personnel and increase expenses. There would be 10 new delivery trucks to purchase in the coming weeks, and 40 full time employees would be needed to produce the additional product and coordinate deliveries.

During the summer months, beginning in late April and lasting until the end of September, Bubba's Frozen Lemonade operated 125 mobile lemonade stands in the Myrtle Beach area. Many of them located on the beach, and others in various hotel oceanfront pool areas across the Grand Strand, seven days a week. In addition, there were lemonade stands located in some of the commercial shopping malls and at several of the golf courses scattered across the South Carolina coast.

It was not unusual for a lemonade stand salesperson to sell 200 to 300 Bubba's Frozen Lemonades on a warm summer day. Easily clearing between $200 to $300 per day in tips alone, plus the hourly wage each stand attendant received from the company. It didn't take long for word to get out among the locals and the college kids that a summer job with Bubba's Lemonade was a great deal. To spend the summer at the beach, working a lemonade stand out in the fresh air and sunshine all day and make that kind of money. What college kid wouldn't kill for that kind of a part time summer job? So, the competition for the lemonade stand attendants job was intense.

In addition to the sales jobs operating the lemonade stands, the company needed delivery drivers to service the stands daily, and make deliveries to local restaurants and nightclubs.

In minor league baseball, players generally earn the minor league minimum. The big money contracts are typically paid to high draft choices, which are only a few of the players. Many minor leaguers take on part time jobs to supplement their incomes. It was not uncommon for Bubba's Frozen Lemonade to have 20 to 30 Seahawk players on their payroll at any given time during the baseball season.

While Steve managed the business side of the operation, Charlie helped coordinate the hiring of lemonade stand employees and delivery drivers which included several Seahawk players. Most of the baseball players made deliveries during the morning, then went from work at the lemonade company to the ballpark for practices and games later in the afternoon. In the minors, it's not good for players to have all day with nothing to do. Having a job that required the players to be somewhere with the responsibility of a job where they can make some extra money, helped keep the guys on a schedule and limited the time they could be involved in other things which might get them into trouble off the field. So, the Seahawks management was in favor of the arrangement.

In addition to helping coordinate the delivery personnel, Charlie had served as a marketing representative for the company since its inception. As a former Most

Outstanding Player Award winner, Charlie was a well-known sports figure across the country. Charlie's affiliation with the company opened the doors for many business meetings. Having Charlie as a marketing rep allowed Steve to set up business meetings with restaurant owners, nightclub managers, grocery stores and hotel managers that would never have happened if Charlie were not present in the room once the meetings started. Steve's legal knowledge of contracts and business savvy, and Charlie's reputation as a former League All Star was a great business combination.

"Hey Charlie," Steve said, "when will Romero and the rest of the guys be getting in for spring training?"

"They will be here Friday. Our first practice is two weeks from Monday," Charlie replied. "I told them to come on into the warehouse Friday morning at 8:30 and we would go over our summer delivery schedule with them and get all their driver's license information for insurance purposes and their personnel forms filled out."

"How many guys do we have on the delivery roster? We need to get that finalized in the next couple of weeks," Steve asked.

"I have 23 players scheduled for deliveries and I have an additional 18 college students signed up as of today," replied Charlie. "I would like to find 5 more just so we have some flexibility in case someone can't make it to work one day. Hopefully I will get those positions filled this week."

"Hey, while we are talking about the baseball players, how many of the guys will be here next Saturday for the Bubba Ball Day at the ballpark? I would be willing to pay them $250 a piece for the day if they want to help with the baseball clinic. Is Romero going to be available for that? I have had several folks ask me if he would be there?" Steve asked.

"He will be there. He told me he wanted to help with that again. And I talked with Jeff Hamm, and he told me the AAU 16 and under team will be there as well. I am thinking we will have 15 players and 25 of the AAU kids there, plus me, you and some of our Seahawk's management and maintenance staff. So, we should be in good shape with that.

"How many kids do we have signed up to attend?" Charlie asked.

"Last I looked we had 113 kids signed up for the morning clinic, and 43 children in the afternoon," Steve said.

"Wow that is a great turnout," Charlie replied.

Bubba Ball was a non-profit funded by the lemonade company. Its mission was to introduce baseball to underprivileged kids and children with disabilities. At a Bubba Ball event the Seahawks' players would give an instructional clinic free of charge for any child 13 and under in the morning. Then in the afternoon, Seahawk Stadium hosted an event for special needs children where the players signed autographs and helped kids to run the bases and participate in other activities. Each child was given a Seahawks jersey with their name on it as well. These events were held once a month during the summer. They had become one the largest charitable events in the Myrtle Beach area.

In addition to the Bubba Ball events, Bubba's Lemonade also sponsored a 16-under AAU travel team which played across the eastern United States.

Giving back to the community was important to Steve. He had never met his father and had little knowledge of his mother either. Having grown up in the foster care system, Steve had a heart for at risk youth. After graduating high school, he worked his way through college. Once he graduated college, he entered the army where he attended law school on the GI Bill. After serving his term in the military, he had located to Myrtle Beach.

Charlie and Steve met in Myrtle Beach 10 years earlier. Neither of them was married at the time. In their younger wilder days, they were fixtures in the Myrtle Beach nightclubs and bars. Steve started a fledgling one-man law practice, while Charlie rehabilitated his arm after Tommy John surgery.

The two became fast friends.

Then six years ago, after Steve had given up his law practice to manage the lemonade business, he met Claire Reynolds. Claire, a talented free-lance artist, specializing in watercolor portraits of children and seaside paintings, was the daughter of Jack Reynolds, one of the largest commercial real estate developers in the state. Rumor had it that Jack had moved to Myrtle Beach in the early eighties with barely a dollar to his name. Now, 40 some odd years later, he was said to be the largest owner of condominiums, hotels and retail shopping centers on the Grand Strand.

8

It was just before sunrise as Loraine laced her running shoes and walked downstairs. She reached in the refrigerator and grabbed an orange and a bottle of water, then walked out onto the balcony of her 11th floor oceanfront high rise condominium. It was a beautiful clear morning, as Loraine sat down in a deck chair, eating her orange and preparing mentally for her morning run.

Within the next few minutes Loraine finished her breakfast, grabbed a lightweight sports jacket from the closet and exited the condo door. She then skipped the elevator, and half jogging took the eleven flights of stairs until she reached the ground floor of the hotel. Once she reached the ground floor, she walked out toward the rear of the hotel for some light stretching. After her stretching was complete, she began to jog along the beach, the ocean on her left, and lines of high-rise hotels to her right. Loraine now increasing her pace headed south along the shoreline.

Loraine had been to the ocean many times before. But this was her first experience living in the south for an extended period. It did not take long for Loraine to embrace the beauty and serenity of waking up and going to bed at night near the ocean.

For the next 30 minutes Loraine ran three and one-half miles along the beach, working up an intense sweat. Once her run was complete, she took a seat on one of the wooden plank beach access decks. As she sat there alone, the sea breeze blowing against her skin, tossing her long black hair haplessly behind her, she counted her blessings. The beauty of it all. She was in a new place, a new job. Her career prospects and a bright future lay before her. She had a lot to be thankful for, and she knew it.

After twenty minutes or so, Loraine took her shoes off and walked down the decking and back toward the dunes. Once exiting the dunes, she casually walked out onto the sandy white beach, then at the edge of the sand where the ocean waters meet the shore, she stood there quietly for a few minutes. Admiring the majesty of God's creation, she turned left and walked back along the shoreline, water lapping now at her feet. With the ocean to her right, the sun rising in the east, Loraine made her way back to her apartment, where she quickly jumped in the shower, preparing for her workday.

Within the hour Loraine had reached the office where she met Doris and the other ladies.

"Doris, is the sound system in place and live on the field?" Loraine asked.

"Yes, the sound crew was out early this morning and tested it, we are good to go," Doris replied.

For the next 30 minutes, the ladies worked in the office, coordinating the day's event schedule one last time, making sure all the children's jerseys were accounted for, labeled and in order. There would be a Seahawks ball cap and jersey for every participant in the morning's instructional clinic and another for all the afternoon children and their parents who would be attending the meet and greet program with the players.

This was the first Bubba Ball event of the season. It was Loraine's first time hosting a baseball organization event as well, so she wanted to make sure everything went smoothly.

It was 9:30am when Loraine approached the on-field microphone stand where she greeted the 300 plus attendees, volunteers, parents and local dignitaries in attendance.

"Good morning and thank you all for coming out this morning to our first Bubba Ball event of the season. I would like to give a special thanks to Steve Wilson, who is here today representing Bubba's Frozen Lemonade, our corporate sponsor for today's event. A special welcome to our mayor and city council members who are in attendance today and thank you to all our volunteers who have made this event possible."

After Loraine's introduction, the baseball clinic began. For the next two and one-half hours, kids from across the Myrtle Beach and South Carolina coastal area were given instructions from the Seahawks players and their 16-Under AAU team. Once the morning session was over there was a barbecue lunch provided for all the attendees, co-sponsored by the beverage company and the Seahawks. This was Loraine's first experience with a southern style pig picking.

"Loraine, be sure and get some of those ribs on your plate with some slaw, boiled potatoes and hush puppies," Doris instructed as Loraine went through the buffet line beside her.

"I don't know if I can eat all that Doris," Loraine replied.

"Come on Loraine," Jean said. "Lord have mercy girl. You are in the south now; we need to put some meat on those bones of yours. Go ahead and eat what you want. You're young, you can work that off later. You need to try some of those barbecue pork ribs. You only live once!"

After making her way through the pig picking line, with a substantial portion of ribs, pulled pork, slaw and hush puppies on her plate, Loraine, along with Doris and Jean, walked toward a picnic table in the stadium concourse where Steve Wilson and his wife Claire, along with Claire's father, Jack Reynolds were sitting.

"Mind if we join y'all?" Doris asked as the three ladies approached the table.

"No, please do," Steve replied. Motioning for the three women to take a seat.

"Loraine, this is my wife Claire, and my father-in-law, Jack Reynolds," Steve continued. "Claire, Jack, you already know Doris and Jean."

"Yes, it is nice to see you all again Jean and Doris, and it is nice to get to meet you Loraine," Claire said. "I have heard a lot of good things about you Loraine. It's nice to have you in Myrtle Beach for the summer."

For the next 45 minutes Claire, Doris and Jean filled Loraine in on some of the local shops, restaurants and tourist attractions. Then as is often the case when meeting someone for the first time, the conversation went from casual to more personal inquiries, as the subject of relationships was discussed.

"So, tell me Loraine," Jack asked, "there must be a handsome young man in your life? A beautiful young lady like yourself. You have a special someone back in Chicago?" Once this question was asked, everyone at the table's antennas perked up.

"No. I don't have a special guy back home," Loraine replied.

"Really?" Doris replied. "That's hard to believe. We will have to do something about that Loraine."

"Yes," Jean said. "Oh, Loraine. There are hundreds of handsome eligible men coming and going here in Myrtle Beach during the summer months and plenty of single eligible men here in town. We will find you a great guy in no time, won't we Doris?"

"Yes," mumbled Doris, while chewing on a pork rib, nodded in agreement. "We will work on that."

"I don't think that's for me right now, Doris," Loraine said. "I have a lot on my plate with this new job, and I will be going back to Chicago at the end of the season. A summer relationship is not the kind of complication I am looking for right now."

Later, once lunch was complete the players took back to the field and spent the remainder of the afternoon with the special needs children, doing various on-field activities and signing autographs and posing for photos with the morning and afternoon session participants and their parents. After the days activities concluded and the fans left the ballpark, Doris, Loraine and Jean, along with the maintenance crew stored away the sound system.

In the end it was just Doris and Loraine alone in the office.

"It's hard to imagine that you don't have a steady boyfriend, Loraine," Doris said. "I know you must have had lots of opportunities working in New York and Chicago."

"I have had a couple of pretty serious relationships, but for one reason or another they didn't pan out. I used to think I would like to find the right guy and get married someday. Maybe have a family. But for now, trying to get ahead in my career is my top priority."

"I guess it is different pursing a career the way you have," Doris said. "Living in New York and modeling, then moving to Chicago with the baseball organization. I suppose that is a fast-paced lifestyle, a lot different than living in a place like Myrtle Beach. When I graduated from college and got a job with the Seahawks here, I was engaged. Before you know it, we had a couple of kids, and they became my priority. I can't imagine my life without my kids.

"Do you ever get lonely Loraine? Living by yourself and not having kids and a husband?" Doris asked.

"Yes, I get lonely sometimes. And there was a time when I was younger that I thought more about getting married and having children. Many of my friends back in Chicago are married and have children. They seem to be happy. When I am around their kids, and I see them together I sometimes wish I had a child of my own. But so far, I have not met the kind of man who I would want to spend the rest of my life with. I thought I had met the right guy once or twice. Got my hopes up maybe I could have a future with a man. But like I said, those relationships didn't work out and the breakups were hard. I am not anxious to go through something like that again.

"I have dated some guys off and on in the past couple of years. But the right guy has not come along for me yet. And this summer, being here for the baseball season and knowing I am going back to Chicago at the end of the summer, I want to keep my life as uncomplicated as possible."

9

It was one o'clock in the afternoon the following Monday, when Charlie and the rest of the Seahawks team met in the Seahawks dugout for their first practice of the season. Team manager, Joe Starling addressed the team.

"Gentlemen, it's great to see all of you today, and to be out here at the ballpark again. For some of you guys who are returning from last year's team it's good to have you back in Myrtle Beach. For you new guys, and we have 23 new players on this year's initial 35-man roster, I would like to welcome you to Myrtle Beach.

"A few ground rules before we get started. You are professional athletes, and I expect you to behave in a professional manner on and off the field. If you have a personal problem that needs to be dealt with and you need to be excused from a practice, game or team meeting, I expect to be told about it before hand. Understood?"

"Yes, sir coach," the players acknowledged as they nodded their heads in agreement.

"Now, I expect all of you guys to be working diligently to develop your skills. Some of you may progress up the system to the big leagues before this season is over if you work hard and play well. Others may move down to a lower-level team before year's end or be traded to another organization. That's how things go in the minor leagues. Playing professional baseball is a business, and we are all judged by our performance on and off the field. But whatever the situation, I expect all of you, to conduct yourself as a professional while you are here in Myrtle Beach and when we are on the road. The quickest way to having to find a job outside of baseball, is to embarrass the organization and yourself by doing something crazy off the field.

"Now let's form three calisthenics lines out in left field, and Coach Ellis will get practice started."

For the next 15 minutes Coach Ellis put the players through some light stretching drills. Once that was over the players formed lines in groups of two and began to throw baseballs back and forth to each other loosening up their arms. As this was happening, introductions amongst the players were taking place, as the returning players met their new teammates for the first time.

In the baseball world, players and rosters change from season to season. The beginning of the baseball season is never the same for any team because every team's roster is made up of different players from year to year.

Once the stretching and warmups concluded, the position players and the infield and outfielders spread across the field, shagging ground balls and fly balls, as they one at a time rotated through the line-up taking batting practice. Meanwhile Charlie and the teams other 11 pitchers, along with their four catchers, moved into the bull pen area for pitching practice.

As the action was happening on the field, Doris Thomas and the three other ladies who worked in the Seahawks administrative office, Helen Green from accounting, Jean Hurt from promotional sales and Kelly Lund from concessions, were looking out the office windows, sizing up this year's talent.

"I tell you what, I love the start of baseball season," Doris said.

"Yes, no matter how old I get, the baseball players year after year, they stay the same!" Helen replied. "Tell me Doris, is Romeo back with the team this year?"

"Yes, he is Helen," Jean continued. "He's down there with the pitchers, wearing the yellow t-shirt. See him over there?"

"I see him now," Helen said. "That is one beautiful man! I am so glad he is back this season."

"I have daughters his age," Kelly said laughingly. "He's out of my league now, but it is still fun thinking about being 22 again! If I were single and had the girlish figure I once had, I would be making a play for that boy!!" Kelly continued now laughing out loud.

"Romeo is a pretty thing," Doris agreed. "But that Charlie Pace still does it for me. He may be a little older than Romeo, but don't you know Good Time Charlie has lots of experience. Knows how to treat a lady if you know what I mean?" All four of them laughed loudly pointing out the window at their favorite players, continuing to evaluate the on-field talent.

Hearing the laughter out in the lobby, Loraine quietly made her way out into the lobby behind them. Gingerly she approached the four ladies, and silently chuckled as their talent evaluation and rating of the players continued.

"Ladies, we have at least 5 solid, bonified 10's on this roster. And 5 more potential 9's I'd say girls. Would you agree?" Doris asked the others.

"I'd say so," Loraine chimed in, startling the other ladies as they all now roared with laughter and giggles.

"Lord have mercy, Loraine!" Doris exclaimed, laughing so hard now she had tears in her eyes. "You can't sneak up on us like that. You liked to have scared me half to death!"

"Well, I heard all the commotion and it sounded like you ladies were having such a good time over here, I felt left out," Loraine replied. "What exactly is it that you girls were doing? I think I can guess."

"Well," Kelly said, "it's the first day of practice and we are just admiring the team, from a female point of view. Checking out the roster so to say. It's a little more difficult now, since the weather is a little cooler, long sleeves and long pants and all. But once the season gets going and the warmer weather comes and the guys go to shorts and t-shirts, or better yet, shorts and no shirts, we try and keep an eye on them every chance we get during practice." The four of them roared in laughter again.

"Yeah," Doris continued. "This is one of the major benefits of working for the Seahawks. Hope you don't mind, Loraine? This is sort of a right of passage for us girls in the administrative offices, first day of practice every season."

"No, I don't mind," Loraine replied. "As a matter of fact, I'll help you with your player rankings since I'm already here anyway. Let's see what we have to look forward to this season from an 'eye candy' perspective."

For the next hour or so Loraine, Doris and the rest of the gang hooped and hollered laughingly as they made their assessments about the prospects for this year's Seahawks roster. It was the first time Loraine had spent time with the ladies in the office on a personal level. Loraine was a huge hit with the girls.

Then around 4 pm, once practice broke for the day. Charlie came up to the administrative offices for a visit.

"Doris, is Loraine available?"

"I think so Charlie. Sit down a minute and I'll see."

A few minutes later Loraine came out to meet Charlie and the two of them went back into Loraine's office for a chat.

"Charlie, it's nice to see you again. Tell me what's on your mind," Loraine asked, hoping Charlie had changed his mind about the documentary.

"I wanted to come by and talk with you about our meeting the other day, Loraine. I have been thinking about our meeting, and I felt like I owed you an apology. I may have seemed a bit distant, or rude when we talked, and I didn't want to leave it that way."

Hearing that Loraine began to get her hopes up, that Charlie had changed his mind.

"That's not a problem, Charlie. I'll admit, I was a little confused by the way our conversation ended," she replied.

"That's what I wanted to talk with you about. I know my reaction may have taken you by surprise. But I have my reasons for not wanting to do the documentary, and I would prefer to keep those to myself. That is not a reflection on you, Loraine. I enjoyed our visit and getting to speak with you. And I am very appreciative of what the network and the baseball organization are trying to do. It is flattering to be considered for this. But for me, at this time in my life, I'd like to keep my personal life personal, as much as I can anyway. I hope you understand.

"I have been thinking about what you told me." Charlie continued, "that part of the reason you were sent here this summer was to work with me and the network on this documentary. I did not want to put you in a delicate position with the organization if I were not to agree to do the documentary.

"I have known Herb Volkmann ever since I signed with Chicago. He was Director of Player Personnel with the baseball organization when I signed my first major league contract. Herb and my family, we have been good friends ever since. I would not want my decision to negatively affect you or your career in any way. So, I would be happy to call and speak with Herb if you like? To assure him that you were courteous and very professional when we met. I'm sure he knows that you would be professional about this situation. But I will be happy to tell him my decision personally, so you don't have to. If that would be better for you?"

As Charlie was speaking, genuinely expressing his concern for Loraine's feelings, and offering to speak with Mr. Volkmann on her behalf, Loraine could see why Doris had told her earlier that Charlie Pace was a great guy. Working in professional sports in Chicago, Loraine had come to see the superficial side of many professional athletes.

As an attractive woman in the sports business, she had been approached many times by players and former players with not so noble intentions and expectations. But there was something different about Charlie. Loraine could see an innocence, almost frailty to his personality. The appealing combination of his boyish charm, masculine good looks and his sincerity, surprised Loraine. And although she knew getting involved with a guy nicknamed 'Good Time Charlie' was probably not a good idea, the longer they talked, the more intrigued she became with Charlie Pace.

"Charlie, I appreciate you coming by and telling me that. And I appreciate you offering to speak with Mr. Volkmann on my behalf. But I have already spoken to Mr. Volkmann about this and told him you were not interested in doing the documentary at this time. Although, I would be lying if I told you I am not hoping you may change your mind about that at some point during the season. But as for me, Mr. Volkmann assured me he respected your opinion and that your decision as to whether or not to do the documentary would not affect my career with the baseball organization. As far as I am concerned, I will not bring this documentary up again. If it is something you would like to do at some point and you change your mind about that, great.

If not, I understand. Your reasons are you own, and I will respect your decision.

"Mr. Volkmann did tell me that he would be spending some time here evaluating players in the next few weeks and he may ask you about the documentary again. But I will leave that up to the two of you to discuss further."

As the two of them sat there, casually speaking together for a second time, it was easy to see there was a chemistry developing between them. Charlie had been interested in Loraine from the moment they first met. Sitting there looking at her now, his infatuation with her continued to grow. Loraine was a sophisticated, lovely young woman, who presented herself in a calm, confident demeanor. Charlie was impressed. And as he listened to her, he became more and more uncomfortable. He wanted to see her again. He could no longer hide his interest. So, he decided it was time to put his intentions about Loraine on the table and see what happened.

"I'm glad we had a chance to talk, I feel better about things now," Charlie said. Sensing that their second meeting was about to end, he didn't want to leave. He wanted their conversation to continue, but what he had come there to say had been said. It was time for his next move.

Charlie stood up, "Well, thanks for taking time out to let me come speak with you Loraine," Charlie said.

Then Loraine stood and extended her right hand to Charlie, "You're welcome, Charlie," she replied.

Once their hands touched, and their eyes met, they both began to smile. Neither of them attempting to deny something was happening here.

"Listen Loraine, I have enjoyed visiting with you again. And if you're interested, I would like an opportunity to spend some more time with you, to get to know you better away from the ballpark. Would you be interested in getting together again and let me take you out to dinner?"

"This is a bad idea," Loraine was thinking, *"steady now Loraine. Be smart here."*

"It's the least I can do since I put you in this awkward position by not doing the documentary," Charlie said.

"But he is so nice and oh my God when he smiles and looks at me that way?" Loraine thought to herself as her self-control was being tested to the max.

"I appreciate you understanding my hesitancy to do the documentary." Charlie continued, "and besides, I'm sure by now you can tell that I am interested in getting to know you better. Away from the ballpark."

"Are you asking me out on a date Charlie?" Loraine asked, a*lthough of course she knew that he was.*

"Yes, I am," Charlie replied.

After an extended smile and a slight pause, Loraine answered.

"I don't normally date ballplayers. And this may not be the smart thing to do, since we are working together. But yes, Charlie, I would like to have dinner with you."

"How about tomorrow at seven? I'll pick you up at your place and I'll take you to my favorite restaurant and we will have dinner and some wine and get to know each other a little better."

"Seven is perfect, Charlie. I'll be looking forward to it."

10

It was 6:00 pm when Loraine exited the shower. Wrapping a towel around her shapely 5-foot 9-inch frame, her wet black hair dripping on her shoulders, she grabbed a bottle of wine and a glass off the kitchen counter and headed out onto the balcony of her apartment. It was a warm night for March as Loraine sat there wondering what she was thinking when she agreed to have dinner with Good Time Charlie Pace.

Loraine understood why she said yes when Charlie asked her out. She was an attractive, single young woman in her early thirties. She was a big girl. This was not her first rodeo where men are concerned. She could take care of herself no question about that. And there was the obvious attraction between them. Charlie was a single, athletic, good-looking guy who was nice to her, would treat her well. What woman isn't looking for a man like that?

Charlie was intelligent, sincere, he checked off all the boxes Loraine was looking for in a man. But the timing was bad.

Loraine knew she would not be staying in Myrtle Beach after the summer, and she worked with Charlie. She did not want to get involved in an office romance or have a summer fling with a ball player and news of that get back to the baseball organization in Chicago. She wanted to be seen as a professional businesswoman, taken seriously in her career. Getting involved with a minor league ball player was the last thing she had on her mind when she came to Myrtle Beach for the summer.

So, as Loraine sat there looking out toward the ocean, her hair drying in the warm evening breeze, she decided she would be cordial and polite tonight on her date with Charlie. But no matter how it went, or how much she may enjoy herself, or how much she was interested in Charlie Pace, this would be their first and last date. She would not risk her promotion in Chicago over a relationship with Charlie Pace or any other man this summer. She would focus on the finish line. The sales managers job in National Sales with the baseball organization. Her love life would just have to wait until she went back to Chicago, promotion in hand.

It was 6:55 when Charlie pulled his Jeep into the oceanfront condominium parking deck. Wearing a pair of tan wrangler jeans, leather lace up boots, flannel shirt and denim jacket, Charlie parked the jeep on the third floor of the garage and headed to the elevator on his way up to Loraine's apartment. A minute before 7, Charlie knocked on Loraine's door.

"You're right on time Charlie, I like that," Loraine said as she opened the condominium door, wearing her favorite pair of white designer jeans, and a tightly fitting red sweater.

"Well thank you Loraine," Charlie replied. "And you sure look nice tonight."

"Thank you, Charlie."

As they were about to exit the door Charlie suggested, "Loraine you might want to take a light jacket with you, the nights in March on the coast can get cool and breezy once the sun goes down."

So, Loraine reached in the closet next to the door and after taking a black waist length leather jacket from the closet, she and Charlie exited the building.

For the next 20 minutes Charlie and Loraine chatted as they made the drive up Hwy 17 Business toward North Myrtle Beach. Once they reached the North Myrtle Beach Marina, Charlie and Loraine entered the sound front restaurant located on the intercoastal waterway where they had a 7:30 reservation.

"This is my favorite place to eat on the grand strand," Charlie said as they made their way through the restaurant entrance.

Every head turned in their direction as Loraine walked through the crowded restaurant to their table located in the back corner of the restaurant, with windows lining the outer walls, overlooking lines of sailboats and yachts gently bobbing on the water tied in their marina slips.

"Do you eat here often Charlie?" Loraine asked.

"Yes, I do. Like I was saying, this is my favorite restaurant. I have lived here in a townhouse at the marina for the last several years. I eat here all the time. Mostly alone."

"Before coming to Myrtle Beach, I had no idea how large the Myrtle Beach area is." Loraine continued, "there are so many restaurants and retail stores. Doris told me it was over 60 miles from where North Myrtle Beach begins and South Myrtle Beach ends. And this marina, wow, it is beautiful at night. There are so many amazing spots on the water here. With so many great choices, how did you choose to live at this marina Charlie?"

"When I first moved here after my elbow surgery," Charlie replied, "I was looking for a quiet place. After living in Chicago for three years I was ready for a slower paced lifestyle. Growing up in St. Petersburg our family did not have a lot of money. We were a middle-class family. Lived in a small suburban area, nothing like downtown Chicago. Living near the coast growing up, I loved the water and always wanted to live on the water one day. This place is quiet. You would never know it was here unless you come here by boat or drive your car here to get in your boat. I like the ocean, but the sound side and intercoastal waterway are more private. Privacy was something I was looking for when I moved here from Chicago."

"Growing up in Chicago and then going to college and working in New York," Loraine replied, "I like the hustle and bustle of the city. I like the nightlife. The parks, restaurants, shopping malls. I was surprised that Myrtle Beach had so many restaurants, the shopping and the beach. I was not expecting there to be so many things to do here."

It wasn't long before their waiter brought their food and a bottle of wine. For the next hour and a half Charlie and Loraine traded information about themselves. Loraine, like Charlie, was a middle-class kid, trying to make it in the world. She had grown up in a large city, surrounded by wealth and privilege she could never possess. She knew as a woman working in the sports business, that while her good looks opened many doors, to be taken seriously she needed to be always on guard where relationships with men were concerned. Men were always approaching Loraine, asking her out on dates and offering to take her places. It had gotten to the point where Loraine was guarded when it came to handsome men. She had had so many disappointments before that she was very leery of letting her guard down with anyone. And she told Charlie as much as they ate their meal and finished their bottle of wine.

Charlie understood Loraine's concerns. After all, being a professional athlete for the past 16 years, he had experienced the good, the bad and the ugly of the sports world. He knew the stereotypical way many male athletes viewed an attractive woman. So, he understood Loraine's reservations about being involved with an athlete, especially since she was working in the baseball organization.

But the more Loraine told Charlie about herself, the more interested Charlie became in her. So, as they continued to talk, Charlie told Loraine about some painful memories he had not spoken to anyone about in a long, long time.

"I understand your reservations about relationships, Loraine. Have you ever been married?"

"No, I have not," Loraine replied.

"I was married when I was back in Chicago. You may have known that already. I was twenty-one when I got married. It lasted two years. Then once I injured my arm and after the surgery, I was rehabilitating here, and she was working in Chicago. Long distance relationships. Very hard to make that work. Soon, our marriage ended, and she was dating another guy. Another athlete in the Chicago area, a hockey player. I never had liked hockey," Charlie smiled as he continued.

"That was a difficult time for me. I was injured. Physically and emotionally. For the first time in my life, I was not able to play baseball or any other sport for that matter. I like water sports, swimming, kayaking. With my arm surgery I had to limit my arms mobility until it healed. So, I had a lot of time on my hands with little if anything to do. I was bitter about that for a long time. I made some poor personal decisions during those years."

"I can understand how you would feel that way Charlie, those are very difficult situations to deal with," Loraine replied.

"It took me a long time to begin to trust in things again after all that. Up until that point in my life things had come easily to me. I never really separated who I was as a ballplayer, from who I am as a person. When I could no longer play ball, the way people treated me changed. My worth in some people's eyes, was tied up in what I could do, only in how I could perform. I lost my wife and many others who I thought were my friends when all that happened.

"Have you ever considered marriage Loraine? Is the idea of children and family in your future?" Charlie asked.

"I hope so. It's not where my focus is now. As a single woman I understand the need to provide for myself. Consequently, my job and establishing my career is what I am focused most on now. What about you Charlie? Is being married something you would consider again?"

"Yes. I want to get married again."

"Really, after what happened before? You are willing to put yourself out there again like that?" Loraine asked.

"Yes, I want to get married, settle down. Have a family, some kids. I absolutely want that. I wanted those things when I was married before. I have great parents. I want those same sorts of relationships my parents have. To have a wife, children. Yes, I want to be married again one day."

As the night went on the couple continued to talk about work, baseball, family, friendships and other life experiences. It was nearly midnight when they finished their conversations and headed out into the parking lot for the drive back to Loraine's condominium.

Once they reached Loraine's condominium, Charlie parked the jeep and he and Loraine headed upstairs. When they reached Loraine's door, there was an awkward moment of silence. The moment at the end of a first date. Will there be a goodnight kiss? Will there be a second date?

"I had a really nice time tonight." Charlie continued as he moved a little closer to Loraine, "and I would like to see you again."

"I had a good time too," Loraine replied. Then she nervously continued. "Charlie, I really like you, and under other circumstances I would be absolutely interested in seeing you again. But since we are working together and knowing that I am going to be leaving the area moving back to Chicago once the summer is over, I am not sure us dating is a good idea."

"I see," Charlie replied as he moved closer to Loraine.

"It's not that I don't want to see you again," said Loraine. "Or that I didn't enjoy our date tonight. I just don't want to complicate things. You understand, don't you?"

"Yes, I understand. You don't have to explain yourself. I can see where dating a ball player while you are here just for the summer might cause you some issues. But before I leave, there is one thing I need to know Loraine."

"What's that Charlie?"

"This," Charlie said as he leaned in and gently kissed Loraine. Loraine was pleasantly surprised by the kiss. She did not pull away. She wanted the kiss, even though she was uneasy about seeing Charlie again.

"I have been thinking about kissing you since we first met," Charlie said as he gently kissed Loraine again. "And since it doesn't look like we will be going out again, I wanted to know what it would be like to kiss you. It was nice."

"Yes, it was Charlie."

"Sometimes Loraine, the best things in life come our way when we least expect them. I had a good time tonight, and I would like to see you again, to see where this goes. If you change your mind about a second date, let me know."

11

For Loraine, the next two weeks were a blur. Seahawk Stadium was buzzing from early morning until late in the evening as the office staff and maintenance crew worked to get everything ready for the season opener against the Greenville Bulldogs. After Loraine's morning run, she would typically be at the ballpark by 8 am and sometimes not leave work until after 9 in the evening, with barely time for a takeout lunch and dinner. Loraine understood that without the documentary, her job performance would be judged solely on her management of the Seahawks home attendance and revenues for the summer.

For the past several years the Seahawks had led the Coastal League in attendance. Myrtle Beach being the vacation destination it has become over the past 20 years helped the Seahawks draw huge crowds for a minor league baseball team. It was not unusual even on a weeknight, for the Seahawks to sell out their stadium seating with standing room only in the stadium concourse.

With the National Sales Manager's job on the line, there was immense pressure on Loraine to live up to or exceed the previous year's attendance records and revenue performance. In addition to those pressures, everything about Loraine's job was new to her. She was meeting and working with all new people, new responsibilities. In Chicago, she was a fashion and merchandising executive. Now Loraine was responsible for personnel issues, full time and part time employees, concessions, advertising, field maintenance, on field promotions, stadium upkeep.

And the fact of the matter was, Loraine knew very little about the game of baseball. She liked watching it with friends and had been to many games. But she knew little if anything about how the game was played, or the ins and outs of what goes on behind the scenes on the field or in the stadium while a game is being played. It was all coming at her at once. She was stressed out about it. Trying so hard to prove herself, she was burning the candle at both ends, and people in the office were noticing.

Doris and the other ladies who worked in the office with Loraine could see that Loraine's demeanor was beginning to sour with all the hours she was working. Loraine was a huge hit with the girls, and they were concerned about her. And as kindhearted women often do, they felt a responsibility to look out for Loraine.

They tried making subtle suggestions to Loraine that she was working too hard and not getting enough rest, and that it was going to catch up with her if she didn't slow down. But to no avail. Loraine kept at it anyway. Loraine was a perfectionist. In the way she dressed. Her work ethic. Her fitness levels. Loraine felt she had to be at her best all the time, she could not accept anything less than perfection. And no one can go on for long in a stressful situation behaving that way.

After some discussion amongst the ladies in the office, it was decided that Doris would be the woman for the job. To sit down and have a heart to heart with Loraine.

It was a little after 7 pm on a Thursday evening when Doris knocked on Loraine's office door.

"Loraine, I brought you some supper," Doris said as she walked into Loraine's office. "You have got to take a break and eat something. You have been in here with the door closed all afternoon. You need to eat."

"Oh, thank you Doris. Whatever you have there, it sure smells good."

"It's some of that brisket like we had at the cookout the other Saturday, and some slaw, sweet tea and hush puppies," Doris replied. It had been six weeks now since Loraine arrived from Chicago, and during that time she had developed a taste for barbecue and sweet tea.

"I know sweet tea, hush puppies and slaw cannot be on a heart healthy diet plan but it sure tastes good," said Loraine as she tried the brisket. "I appreciate you thinking about me Doris."

"You're welcome, Loraine, besides, I got me a plate too." Doris continued, "do you want some company for dinner? You have been spending too many nights couped up in here alone Loraine. Me and the other girls, we are concerned about you working so many nights straight. You can't go on like this Loraine. The season hasn't even started yet. Once it does, we will be here late into the night some of those evenings we have a ball game. You have got to pace yourself. I'm concerned about you."

"I appreciate it Doris," Loraine replied as she got up from her chair and walked around the desk and gave Doris a hug. "Really, I do. I know I have been in a foul mood lately. I don't mean to be. I'm just anxious about my new job. I want everything to go well and it's a lot of new responsibilities for me."

"Loraine, you remember when we had our first staff meeting, the day you got here. You told everyone you wanted to keep things in place the same way they were the past several years because things were going so well before you got here, you did not want to change a thing. That you would be counting on us to run things this season the way we had in the past."

"Yes Doris, I remember saying that."

"Well, that's what you need to do Loraine. Just what you said. All our staff from last year is back in place. Our maintenance crew is the same. We have the same group of advertisers and public address announcers. The same management people running concessions. We have all the same key people in place as the past several seasons. Things are going to be fine."

"I know that, Doris. You're right. I need to relax. I have confidence in y'all. I do."

"Okay that's good, so what's changed Loraine? Why are you working so many late nights? Why are you so anxious these past two weeks?"

"I'm not really sure, Doris. I am anxious now, for several reasons, I guess. Being in a new place. I miss my routine and my friends back in Chicago. When I go home at night after work now there is no one there. It can be lonely in a new place when you don't know people along with the responsibility of this new job. It is so different than anything I have done before. I am in charge. But really, if it wasn't for everyone else knowing what to do, I would be lost. It makes me uncomfortable to be so dependent on everyone else. It makes me feel out of control, and that makes me anxious."

For the next two hours the two ladies sat there in the office chairs with their barbecue plates resting on top of Loraine's desk talking about fears, dreams, hopes, friendship, trust. The things that make life worth living. Loraine shared her fears as a single woman trying to make it in a man's world. She shared with Doris that she was saddened Charlie was against the documentary and afraid that if he did not change his mind, she may not get the National Sales Manager job in Chicago. But that she told Charlie she would not ask him about it again, even though she wanted to.

She then told Doris about her date with Charlie. She admitted she had a wonderful time, but had told Charlie they should not see each other again since she would be leaving after the summer, and it could be awkward since they were working together. Loraine was lonely. She was scared. She had a lot on her plate. She was anxious. And she wasn't sure how to handle it.

12

The lemonade business was about to get into full swing with the first of April quickly approaching. The beach tourists would be returning soon and that combined with an increased number of golfers traveling to Myrtle Beach to play on the areas 100 plus golf courses, would pack local beaches, hotels and restaurants. The lemonade company historically does seventy-five percent of their business in the summer months from April to September.

In addition to the summer sales increases, there was the new contract Steve had signed with the Food Chain. All of this activity was coming together at the same time. There were 40 plus new full-time employees to train in addition to all the new part time workers manning the lemonade stands on the beaches, hotel swimming pools and at golf courses who needed to be hired and organized. With the additional sales from Food Chain orders, Steve would be adding another 10,000 square feet to the existing warehouse facility.

On the field, the baseball team was taking shape nicely. With Romero and Charlie in the starting rotation and a hand full of other talented young pitchers, the Seahawks had the nucleus of a fine pitching staff. In addition to his pitching duties, Charlie also spent part of his time at the ballpark as an assistant coach working primarily with the other pitchers. After 16 years in professional baseball, and Charlie's reputation as a two time all star and former Most Outstanding Player Award winner, he had instant credibility with the younger players. After all, what aspiring young pitcher would not want to learn all he could from a guy who had led the league in strike outs and ERA in two different major league seasons.

The baseball organization in Chicago had already expressed interest in bringing Romero to Chicago at some point during the season if he continued to perform the way he had the previous year. In addition to Romero, the Chicago front office had high hopes for third baseman Pete Roberts and right fielder Josh Harris. Both of them were young power hitters who the previous year were playing single A ball in Galveston, Texas.

With the Seahawks opener just three days away, Charlie took a personal leave day to attend a business meeting with Steve in Atlanta to do a promotional appearance with the management heads of the Food Chain. Steve's father-in-law, Jack Reynolds, who often traveled with Steve on business meetings, flew Steve and Charlie to Atlanta on his private plane.

Once the trio landed in Atlanta, representatives from the Food Chain met them at the airport. Then they drove to the Food Chain headquarters for the announcement of the deal to a group of the Atlanta business press at a luncheon and press conference.

"It's a great opportunity for Bubba's Frozen Lemonade to be the newest vendor in the Food Chain family," Steve said as the cameras flashed around the room. "We are excited to be moving into the Atlanta beverage market and the 300 plus retail grocery stores across the southern United States and Midwest under the Food Chain umbrella. This partnership will allow our company to expand our work force and create new opportunities for our employees in Myrtle Beach. We appreciate the confidence the Food Chain has shown in our organization, and we expect this to be a long, profitable relationship for the Food

Chain and our owners, managers and employees for many years to come."

After Steve's presentation he and Charlie spent the next two and one-half hours eating lunch and mingling with members of the Atlanta press and Food Chain executives. It did not take long before the questions went from business to sports, with Charlie shaking hands and posing for pictures with nearly every person in the room.

It had been 10 years since Charlie had thrown a pitch in a major league game. But still his name recognition as a former professional baseball player who was a two time All Star and former Most Outstanding Player Award winner resonated with baseball fans everywhere.

As was always the case in these types of events, there were the conversations about his elbow surgery and the staph infection that followed. Well wishers saying they were so sorry when that happened. Fans who said they had seen Charlie pitch in the All-Star game in Atlanta 12 years ago and vividly remembered him striking out the side in the first inning of that All Star game.

Charlie was always obliging when fans asked for handshakes, autographs and posed for pictures at these events. It was part of the job. Charlie's celebrity status opened the doors which often led to many successful and profitable financial arrangements. And now even in his mid-thirties, professional baseball fans could not get enough of Good Time Charlie Pace.

Later that evening on the flight home Steve and Charlie talked about their past and hopes for the future.

"That couldn't have gone any better," Steve said. "Charlie, would you ever have dreamed a few years ago when you and I were making our own drink mixers in your townhouse at the marina, that one day we would be flying in a private jet back to Myrtle Beach from Atlanta after signing a deal with the Food Chain?"

"Never in a million years," Charlie replied. "A lot has changed since then. I never thought I would still be playing baseball, not after the surgery. I could barely lift my arm for two years. When I think about those days, and where we are now, what happened today is a miracle in so many ways."

"Meeting Claire, and her influence on me," Steve continued, "I don't know where I would be if she hadn't come along when she did. You and I, we were both in a dark place back then brother. Now here we are in her father's private plane. I think about where we were then sometimes and wonder how we got here? I was a total mess, and yet, somehow Claire saw some good in me. That angel of a woman loved me anyway. She was my angel sent from God."

"No doubt," Charlie replied, "her influence on you. Taking you under her wing. Encouraging you. Her dad, Jack, the way he invested himself in you. Now you and Claire have a family and two beautiful children together. Claire and Jack, they saved you, and you saved me. It was a miracle."

13

There was not an empty seat anywhere to be found in sold out Seahawks Stadium as Charlie finished his warmup session in the bullpen before the start of the team's first baseball game of the season. Charlie finished the last of his warmup pitches, then grabbed a lightweight Seahawks jacket and slipped it over his right arm to keep it warm as he made his way out of the bullpen slowly walking toward the team's first base dugout.

"You looked mighty good down there, big fella," said a tall slender man in his early sixties, who was standing along the chain link fence separating the field from the stadium concourse as Charlie made his way to the dugout.

"Hey there Dad," Charlie said walking over to the fence, giving his dad a hug and a handshake. "When did you get here?"

"I got into town an hour or so ago. I stopped and got a bite to eat. It's great to see you, son."

"It's great to see you too Dad. Looking forward to you spending the week with me. We are going to play some golf, cook out on the grill, take the boat out, do some fishing."

"That sounds great, son. Well don't let me interrupt your warmup, I don't want to keep you. You have work to do. Go have a great game and I'll see you after. I love you and I am proud of you Charlie."

"Thanks Dad. I love you too. I'll see you after the game."

Soon thereafter, Charlie's dad, Ed Pace, made his way back to his seat behind home plate just as the public address announcer asked the crowd to take off their caps and stand for the singing of the National Anthem.

Meanwhile, Loraine was moving quickly from one area of the stadium to another checking and double checking that everything was in place and going smoothly. Since Doris and Loraine's heart to heart talk in Loraine's office a few days earlier, Loraine had made some progress in settling her nerves and dealing with the stress of her new job. Loraine was more relaxed, as she had made a decision to get out of the office more and trust in her co-workers to do their jobs. That decision had eased the stress in the office and helped Loraine bond closer to Doris and the other folks she worked with.

It was 7:05 pm when Charlie stepped on the mound. He threw his seven warm-up pitches before the catcher threw the ball down to second base, then around the infield the ball went, before the third baseman fired the ball back to Charlie now standing ten feet or so behind the mound. Charlie said a quick prayer before he walked on top of the pitcher's mound and toed the rubber preparing to throw the game's first pitch.

Over the next seven innings Charlie allowed two hits and one earned run, while striking out eight Greenville batters and walking no one as the Seahawks built a commanding 4-1 lead. Changing speeds and painting the edges of the plate while throwing just 87 pitches. His fastball topping out at a respectable 90-mph. Then in the eighth inning Charlie was replaced by the Seahawk bullpen as they cruised to a 6-2 opening night win.

Behind the scenes, Loraine and her staff managed the concessions, on field promotions and the post-game fireworks without any sort of incident that would cause Loraine or Doris any type of stress whatsoever. Relieving some of Loraine's pregame anxiety and helping her to relax and trust that things as Doris said, would be okay going forward.

Once the game ended and the fireworks concluded the team met briefly and discussed the night's performance and organized the plan for the next day's afternoon home game. After their short team meeting, Charlie walked out the stadium side gate where his father Ed was waiting to greet him.

"That was some mighty fine pitching tonight young man," Ed said as Charlie walked toward him. "You made that look mighty easy. You really pitched a nice game tonight, son."

"Thanks Dad," Charlie replied. "Everyone played well tonight. We played well defensively, and the bats were solid behind me. Made my job a lot easier. What did you think about Roberts and Harris? Aren't they impressive young ballplayers?"

"Yes, they are. Both will do well in the majors once they get there. That home run Josh Harris hit in the first inning was a rocket. And Pete Roberts looks very smooth at third base. You could see he has great speed when he ran out that standup triple in the eighth inning. Those two are everything you said they would be. I don't think either of those boys will be playing for the Seahawks in Myrtle Beach when the season ends. I think they will both be playing in Chicago with the big team before the year is over."

"I agree Dad. Romero pitches tomorrow. He has looked great in our practices and the word from Chicago is that all three of them will be called up before the season ends."

"Herb Volkmann told me the last time we spoke," Ed continued, "they have high hopes for this year's team in Chicago. They finished the season last year with a winning record for the third straight season and with the talented young roster they have and these young guys coming up through the system, Herb believes they will be a playoff contender all season. I would love to see the team make the playoffs this year. It's been a long time since we have competed for a championship in Chicago."

"Yes, it has. Hopefully this will be the year Chicago gets over the hump and back in the playoffs."

"Well, I am going to drive on over to your condominium and get my stuff situated and I will see you when you get home Charlie."

"Okay Dad, I'll see you in a bit," Charlie replied.

Ed gave Charlie a hug and headed off to his car while Charlie made his way around the parking lot to the players parking area in the back corner of the stadium. Once Charlie reached his Jeep, he found Loraine leaning up against it waiting for him there.

"Isn't this a nice surprise," Charlie said as he walked toward Loraine. "How did we do tonight boss?"

"I thought you did good. Honestly, like I told you the other night I don't know a whole lot about baseball, but everyone who does said you did great! We won. So that is good."

"Well, I appreciate your honesty," Charlie said smiling at the thought of Loraine's candid remarks. "It was a good win. Great way to start the season. How did your first night go running the show as a General Manager, Loraine?"

"It went great. Doris and her team did a super job," Loraine replied. "Nothing crazy happened. Thank God. And we had a sellout crowd. Things went very smoothly. I feel a lot better about things now that we have a game under our belts. I learned a lot tonight. Doris has done a great job here. We are lucky to have her."

"Yes, you are lucky to have Doris. She is a good woman for sure. Did I hear you say you've learned a lot lately, Loraine? How so?" Charlie asked as he leaned back against the Jeep arms crossed beside Loraine.

"Well, to be honest, I have been very stressed since I got here," Loraine said, fidgeting a bit. "Like I told you earlier, I don't have a lot of background in baseball. So, I have had to lean on everyone else to do my job and I don't like being unprepared. I like to take control of things more than I should I guess."

"Really, I would have never guessed that about you Loraine," Charlie said sarcastically.

"Ha, ha," Lorraine replied. "Yeah, I can be a bit of a perfectionist at times I know. It's not the first time anyone told me that about myself."

"I see," Charlie replied.

"Well anyway," Loraine continues, "I have been talking with Doris and she has helped me trust in the others more and get out of the office a bit these last few days and she was right about that. We also talked about some other things I was not sure about that were bothering me, and I have decided to listen to her advice and make some other changes that I hope will help as well."

"Other changes?" Charlie asked. "Like what Loraine?"

"I told Doris you and I went out for dinner and that I had a great time," Loraine replied. "But I was concerned about how dating you might affect my job and I was not interested in seeing you again because I was afraid a summer romance would be too much of a distraction. I told her you asked me out on a second date, and I said no because it might be too complicated, with everything else I had going on at work."

"What did Doris say about all that Loraine?"

"She told me if I didn't go out with you again whenever you asked me, I was crazy."

"I see. You know Loraine, Doris is a smart lady. What do you think you should do about that?"

"I think Doris is right," Loraine continued as she moved closer to Charlie and reached forward resting her arms across the tops of his broad shoulders. "I would be crazy not to see you again. I have been thinking about you since we had dinner the other night. I think it was kind of selfish on my part worrying about my job and not giving us a chance. I was afraid of being hurt again. I hope I have not missed my opportunity with you Charlie. I wanted to tell you, that if you would like to go out again, I would appreciate a second date."

"Are you asking me out Loraine?" Charlie asked.

"Yes, I am," Loraine replied.

Charlie slipped his arms around her slender waist, pulling her gently closer to him. "I would love to see you again Loraine."

14

"Good morning, Charlie. You were out pretty late last night," Ed said. "I went to bed about midnight. I was going to wait up for you, but an old man like me, we have to get our rest."

"Yeah, sorry about that dad. Something came up and I got detained at the ballpark for a while. You want to grab some breakfast on the way to the warehouse? Steve is going to meet us there. We have a few things we need to look at before we head over to Pine Lakes to play golf."

"Yeah, that works for me. I have my clubs in the trunk of my car. I am ready to go whenever you are son."

"I want to swing by Flo's and pick up a biscuit for us and Steve on the way dad if that's alright with you."

Before long Charlie and Ed had loaded Ed's golf clubs in Charlie's Jeep and headed to the warehouse. They stopped by Flo's along the way and picked up four sausage and egg biscuits. Once they arrived at the warehouse Steve and Charlie looked over some machinery being installed in the company's facility to handle the increased production necessary to fill the additional frozen lemonade orders, they were now supplying to the Food Chain. Once the work was complete, the three of them drove over to the golf course where they met Jack Reynolds for their 11am tee time.

Over the years as Steve and Charlie's friendship grew, Ed and Charlie had become well acquainted with Jack. Steve was like a son to Jack. Having never met his own father, Steve had great admiration for his father-in-law. Jack had been there for Steve when Steve was a struggling down and out attorney trying to establish himself in the Myrtle

Beach business community. Once Steve and Claire began dating and Jack could see how well Steve treated his daughter, Jack made every effort to support Steve in his personal and professional life. Jack had become a business and personal advisor for Steve. The four men had developed a special bond over the past five years. They had taken regular golf and fishing trips, and traveled together on business trips, ballgames and other sporting events around the country.

During the rest of the week Charlie and Ed played golf, went fishing, spent time at the warehouse, and cooked on the grill. It was a warm week weather wise, so they went to the beach a couple of days as well. Later in the week on Friday afternoon, Loraine took some time off from work and spent the afternoon at the beach with Ed, Charlie, Jack, Claire and Steve, and their two children, John and Sarah.

It was a beautiful day, not a cloud in the sky. A gentle breeze blowing from the south. Temperatures in the mid-eighties. A perfect afternoon to be outside in the sun. As the afternoon progressed Loraine began to see why Charlie wanted children and a family. Being around Claire and Steve and their two children, Loraine began to visualize what it would be like to have a family of her own. Charlie adored Steve and Claire's kids. Seeing Charlie and Ed, playing in the surf with four-year-old John and building sandcastles with two-year-old Sarah, Loraine began to imagine she and Charlie as a married couple with children of their own spending warm summer days as a family at the beach.

Even though they had only known each other for a short while, on this warm spring day at the beach, Loraine began to rethink her priorities. Silly, she thought at first. To be so interested in this man she barely knew. But there was something about Charlie. There was an instant chemistry between them. She felt it the first day they met in her office.

She tried to deny those feelings at first, but the more she was around Charlie, and now seeing him with friends and family, her affection for him grew. Maybe her first instincts were right? Maybe just maybe, it was time for her to trust someone again?

"You have two beautiful children, Claire," said Loraine as she watched Ed, Charlie and John playing in the waves.

"Thank you, Loraine. We are blessed to have two happy, healthy kids," Claire responded. "I am glad you were able to get away from the office and join us today, Loraine. I hope we will be seeing a lot more of you this summer. It's great to have you out here at the beach with us. Steve and I want to have you and Charlie over for dinner one night soon."

"Thanks Claire, I would love that. I have been spending a lot of hours at work lately. More than I should have, I guess." Loraine continued, "it's nice to be out here in the fresh air and sunshine. I feel like a different person these past few days since I have been trying to get away from the office more. I really appreciate you letting me spend time with you and your family, to meet your children. They are adorable."

"You know Loraine, Steve has told me a lot of good things about you. He says he thinks you are really good for Charlie. Steve loves Charlie like a brother," Claire said as she rubbed sunscreen on baby Sarah's back. "Just so you know, one woman to another, Charlie has talked about you, since the two of you met, more than any other woman he has dated in the past six years since I have known him."

"Really?" said Loraine, who of course was pleasantly surprised.

"Yes, he has. When I first met Charlie," Claire continues as she helped Sarah open her fruit punch, "he was in a tough place. He was trying to get over his elbow surgery and he was limited in what he could do physically. Charlie, as I am sure you realize by now, is not the kind of man who can sit around. He had limited use of his right arm at that time, and he was very down about it for several years. It was very hard on him."

"Yes, I know. Charlie and I talked about that on our first date," Loraine replied.

"Charlie told you about that?" Claire responded in surprise as she handed Sarah her sand shovel and bucket. "The first night you went out to dinner?"

"Yes. We talked about a lot of things that first night. It's been a long, long time since I have had a conversation like that with a man," said Loraine as she leaned forward in her beach chair, rubbing sunscreen with both hands on her long slender legs.

"Wow. Charlie never talks about his past with anyone," Claire replied as she leaned back in her beach chair, digging her toes into the warm white sand between her toes. "He is generally, a very private person, very guarded about his feelings. He must be very comfortable when he is with you Loraine, to open up and share his feelings that way. That's wonderful. Since I have known Charlie, he has had dozens of girlfriends. When I first met him and Steve, they were out and about every night. Charlie earned that 'Good Time Charlie' nickname, Loraine," Claire chuckled as she leaned forward and put her hand on Loraine's right shoulder. "That man was out with a different girl every night of the week for a few years there. And any one of them would have killed to be where you are sitting now. Back in Chicago and here for several years here in Myrtle Beach, Charlie lived the devil may care party lifestyle.

"But he is different now. Back then, after his divorce from the weather girl, he never says her name by the way,

76

Loraine," Claire said as she pulled her sunglasses down so Loraine could see her eyes, making the point that the weather girl conversation was off limits whenever she spoke with Charlie about his past. "He just calls her the weather girl. After his divorce from her, he wasn't the kind of guy to be with any woman for very long. But in the past two years or so particularly, Charlie has changed. He's a great guy now. He must be very comfortable with you, for him to trust you enough to tell you those things."

"It was so easy talking with Charlie that first night at the restaurant," Loraine replied as she leaned back in her lounge chair, the sun beaming down on her trim athletic body. "He intently listened to everything I had to say. We were just chatting away, telling each other about various experiences from our past. I told Charlie some things that night over dinner and a bottle of wine, that I haven't spoken to anyone about ever. I told him I had been in a couple of bad relationships, and was leery about getting involved with a man again. I have never told another guy that. It was just something about Charlie. He seemed so honest and sincere. I felt like I could tell him anything. Even personal things after only speaking to him for a short while."

"Did Charlie tell you how he and Steve met? How the lemonade business got started?" Claire asked.

"No, we didn't talk much about his job working for Steve in the lemonade business. I know he likes working for Steve. He tells me about all the great things Steve is doing and how your family's business is growing so fast."

"I see," Claire replied. "That's all Charlie told you about him and Steve's relationship?"

"He did say that Steve had helped him through some rough times. He didn't give me any more specifics than that."

The rest of the afternoon Loraine relaxed in the sun as she watched John and Sarah move in and out of the water. Across the sand, up and down the beach the kids moved constantly, until they had drained all the energy from their tiny bodies. Finally, they collapsed on two towels under an oversized beach umbrella protecting them from the sun. Once the kids fell asleep, Charlie took a seat next to Loraine, his tanned powerful body stretched out next to hers. For the rest of the afternoon, the two couples, along with Ed and Jack, discussed business, baseball, and family. As Loraine sat there, the warm sun on her skin, gentle breeze blowing in her hair, cold beer in her hand, she began to laugh and smile again. For the first time in a long time, Loraine let her guard down. The beautiful, intelligent young woman sitting there on the beach, let herself go a bit. She moved past her feelings of insecurity. She began to believe that good things could happen for her. She began to dream a bit. That she could be in a relationship with an honest man, where two people get along. That she could be a part of a family where people loved and trusted one another. That she could put her trust in a man who would love her for who she is, not for how she looks or how much money she makes. That the fate of the whole world did not have to rest solely on her slender shoulders. That she could trust again.

Over the next several weeks Claire and Loraine met and ate lunch regularly and went on shopping trips together. Loraine and Charlie babysat the children on several occasions. The two couples went out to dinner. Claire introduced Loraine to her friends around town, at the gym, the country club, and the ladies in her Bible study. They went to church together.

As time passed, Loraine began to see why the locals loved living in Myrtle Beach. And maybe just maybe, what Charlie said to her after he kissed her unexpectantly the night of their first date was true. Sometimes the best things in life come our way when we least expect them.

15

"Doris, we have two people who didn't show up for work in the concession stand," Loraine said as she and Doris, walkie talkies in hand, briskly walked beneath the stadium bleachers frantically moving replacement employees in place to cover for the missing workers. "And the ball girl on the third base line fell chasing a ground ball and twisted her ankle. She is going to be alright, but she can't work the foul lines tonight. So, we are three people short, and the game starts in twenty minutes!"

It had been one of those days. Everything that could go wrong had gone wrong. The food delivery of hot dogs and chicken tenders was short two and three cases respectively. The audio system was not working properly. The guy who was supposed to sing the National Anthem before the start of today's 6 pm game called in with a sore throat just an hour before the start of the ballgame. The draft beer delivery was two hours late and it was fifty cent draft beer night. It was crazy. Loraine was losing her mind. Her perfectionist personality simply could not cope with all the last-minute changes. Her perfect pregame plan was falling to pieces before her eyes, and she was about to lose it. But somehow, in the midst of all the drama, Doris remained calm.

"Alright, we are going to move two of the ticket handlers to work the drink stations in concessions. Jean, find a teenager who looks like he knows something about baseball and get him out of the stands and give them a free ball cap and $30 to work the third base line. And let's cue up the recorded version of the National Anthem," Doris calmly stated as she instructed her co-workers into place. "Joe, get $400 out of the petty cash and run over to the Food Lion and buy all the hot dogs and chicken tenders they have. I'll call ahead to the meat department manager and tell him what's going on here at the ballpark. He has helped us out in the past when our food deliveries have run short."

Within the next hour or so, Doris had managed the various crisis beautifully. She was a pro.

"I don't know how you do it Doris. Honestly, you make it look so easy," Loraine said while sipping on a large cup of sweet tea as the drama subsided.

"I've been doing this for 14 years Loraine. There is not much that can go wrong that I haven't seen before in all those years. I try not to worry about it too much."

"I wish I could do that, not worry so much," Loraine said as she sat down in a chair looking out the glass window of one of the stadium's private box lounges lining the top of the Seahawk Stadium grandstand.

"This job, it's still new for you Loraine," Doris replied. "But you are getting more comfortable, aren't you? You seem to be more at ease now. Just think how much you have learned in just the few weeks since you got here. I think you are doing great. Just give it a little time and if something goes crazy, we will figure it out.

"Besides Loraine, now that you have some 'off the field distractions', I thought you would be more relaxed? How is your love life Loraine?" Doris asked as she grabbed a hush puppy off the buffet table in the luxury suite.

"Not bad," Loraine said sipping her sweet tea. Her heart rate now coming back to a more normal range.

"Not bad? Is that all you have to say about it?" Doris asked inquisitively.

"Not bad. You know Doris," Loraine said as she leaned back in her chair smiling broadly now. "I'm not one to kiss and tell. Charlie has his reputation to protect after all. I'll say this, you were right Doris. It was the right thing for me to do, to go out with him again. I am very satisfied with Good Time Charlie. I'll leave it at that."

By this time, down on the field, the baseball game was entering the top of the third inning. This was Charlie's second start of the season. The Seahawks had won three of their first four games entering tonight's ballgame. Charlie had pitched two shutout innings so far, striking out three and allowing just one hit. In the top of the third the Charleston Mud Hens scored two runs on a two-out homerun by their star right fielder Marcello Garcia. Charlie got the next Mud Hen batter out on strikes to end the inning. The Seahawks would go on to score three runs in the bottom of the third inning and two more runs in the bottom of the sixth as they went on to a 7-3 victory. It was Charlie's second win against no losses as he pitched seven complete innings, striking out eight Charleston batters and allowing just two earned runs.

After the game Charlie and Ed grabbed a late meal at the Marina, then they went back to Charlie's townhouse. It was Ed's last night in Myrtle Beach before heading back to St. Petersburg the next morning.

"I never get tired of looking at this view," Ed said as he sat down in a lounge chair on Charlie's back deck, looking out across the intercoastal waterway. "It is so peaceful and quiet out here at night."

"Yes, it is Dad. I love it here. I can't imagine ever living anywhere else," Charlie replied as he leaned back in his wooden deck chair to Ed's left, looking out across the water gently rippling in the distance, Bubba now lying on the wood decking beside him.

"I've had a great week visiting with you son. I would like to come and see you more often, but I don't want to wear out my welcome. You are mighty busy now with baseball and work. And I really like Loraine. You have a lot of good things on your plate now."

"I do. But don't worry about wearing out you welcome with me, Dad. I've had a great week with you here. I'm glad you came. You are welcome anytime."

"I appreciate that son. When you and your brothers were younger, I saw you every day, and back then I was so busy sometimes I took that for granted. But once you all grew up and moved out of the house, I realized how special it was to spend time with you guys. It's not an easy thing for a parent to step back and watch their children move away and make a life on their own and not be able to see them as much as when they were younger.

"The other day when we were at the beach with Steve's kids, that brought back a lot of good memories for me. When your mom and I would take you boys over to the beach and play in the sand. I am very proud of you Charlie. All three of my sons."

"Thanks Dad. I wish I could get back home and see you more often. With my schedule now I am tied up year-round, with baseball and my job in the lemonade business. But you are welcome anytime. I always look forward to your visits."

Over the next two hours Ed and Charlie talked about the years when Charlie and his brothers, Tim and Harry, grew up in the Pace home. Family vacations, sports teams the boys played on. They talked about Tim and Harry's wives and children. Tim and Harry both lived and worked in the St. Petersburg area. Happily married with children of their own now. Ed stayed in close touch with the boys. He tried to be there for them when they needed him, while not interfering. Which is a fine line to walk when you are a father who loves their children the way Ed loved his sons. So as the two men sat there on the deck, looking out at the boats quietly moving along the intercoastal waterway, Ed was waiting for the proper moment to bring up a subject he felt he and Charlie should discuss.

"Charlie, there is something I would like to talk with you about before I leave tomorrow morning."

"Sure Dad. What is it? Is anything wrong with you or mom? Tim and Harry, are they all doing, okay?" Charlie asked as the conversation suddenly seemed more serious.

"No, no Charlie. They are all fine. I wanted to talk with you some more about the documentary piece the Sports Channel wanted to do on you."

"What about it, Dad?" Charlie asked as he shifted around in his chair a bit uncomfortable with where this might be going. "I have decided the documentary isn't something I want to do. That's not for me Dad."

"You're a grown man Charlie. I respect your opinion and you have reasons for your decision I know. But I would like to talk about it some anyway if that's alright with you? I don't want to tell you what to do, but I have some thoughts about it that I would like to talk about if that's okay with you?"

"We can talk about it, Dad. But I don't see me changing my mind about doing it. I don't mind talking about it. And I appreciate your opinion but I don't want you to be disappointed in me if I don't change my mind about this," Charlie said as he made his position on the subject known.

"Fair enough." Ed continues, "I know you have your reasons for not wanting to do it. But I think a lot of good could come from the documentary. You have had some great things happen to you Charlie. You have experienced and done things that other people can only dream about."

"I have Dad. I have had some wonderful experiences and opportunities that I am so thankful for. But I have also experienced some things and done some things I would not wish on anyone. I am not comfortable talking about my past. I am happy where my life is now. I have so much to be thankful for. I don't see the point or the benefit to me to relive that on national television for the whole world to see."

"That's why I want to talk with you about this Charlie. You have a platform to do some good here. I have never been in your shoes, being a public celebrity the way you have been in the past, and still are today. I know it's not easy to be in the spotlight the way you were when you were in Chicago. People watching your every move everywhere you went 24/7. But you have overcome some very difficult things these past few years. I am prouder of you for what you have been through and overcome off the field, than anything you ever accomplished as a player even when you won the Most Outstanding Player Award. I am so proud of you Charlie. The way you have grown and handled yourself as a man. Not just as a ballplayer. I think a lot of people could be inspired by what you have done. The man you have become. This documentary seems to me to be an opportunity to use the difficult things you have faced in your past for good."

"I appreciate what you are saying Dad. I do. But I don't know that I am ready for this. Now, for the first time in a long time, I am becoming more comfortable in who I am again. I spent a lot of years doing some things I am not proud of. And Steve and I, the lemonade business, selling frozen lemonade and drink mixers. How would that affect the business? Steve has worked so hard. He and Claire, they have two small children. How would a documentary affect Steve and his family?"

"I am not trying to tell you what to do Charlie. I understand what you are saying. You have been through a lot. So has Steve. And what you two have done. Where you are now. What you guys have accomplished. It is a miracle.

"Sometimes Charlie, we need to share our stories, so we can be an encouragement to someone who may be struggling with a problem we have faced and overcome. Maybe you could be an example of what can happen when a person believes in miracles.

"Have you talked to Steve about this? This is both of your stories really. If you are worried about how a documentary would affect Steve and the business, maybe you two should talk about it before you make up your mind for certain one way or the other?"

Charlie stood up out of his deck chair and walked over to the wood railing placing his hands on top of the rail, looking out toward the waterway. Ed then stood and walked over beside him, resting his hand on Charlie's left shoulder.

"I don't know if I can do that, Dad," Charlie said fighting back the tears, his painful past flashing through his mind.

"I know what happened to you Charlie, this isn't an easy thing for you to talk about. But I want you to know this, I am so proud of you Charlie. I am proud to be your father. In my mind, what you have overcome and where you are now is something to be very proud of. Whatever you decide to do about this is up to you. I just want you to know I love you and I am proud of you. I needed to tell you how I feel about this as your father. Whatever you decide to do about it now is up to you. I won't bring it up again."

16

For the next 14 days the Seahawks were on the road. During this trip they played a total of 12 games, three games in Dayton Beach, three games in Jacksonville, Florida, three games in Savannah, Georgia and three games in Charleston, SC. Over those two weeks the Seahawks won nine of twelve games pushing their season record to 15-5, putting them in first place in their division. Charlie made three starts during this road trip, winning two games with one no decision. Romero also continued to pitch superbly winning all three games he pitched, striking out a total of 29 batters in his three starts.

During those two weeks while the baseball team was on the road, Loraine got some needed rest. It was the first time since the season began that she was able to have some extended private time to herself and unwind. With the team on the road there were no home games, so Loraine and her staff had some days off to recharge their batteries a bit.

In minor league baseball when teams are playing at home, the management employees often work consecutive days with little or no time off. Since most of the games are played at night, it is not unusual for the management staff to arrive at the ballpark in the morning and not leave until the games are completed and the facility is cleaned and put in order late in the evening. On several nights during the Seahawks opening home series, it was after midnight before Loraine and her staff would finish their duties and leave the ballpark.

As per her normal routine, even on her days off, Loraine would be up early to get her morning run in.

Afterwards, she would go into the office for an hour or so to check her emails and return messages. It had been two months now since Loraine arrived in Myrtle Beach, and the slower lifestyle and warmer weather were agreeing with her. She spent several of her days off lounging around the pool at her condominium and on the beach. Being outside in the sun, her toes in the sand, a cold drink in her hand, Loraine had time to think. And during these two weeks while the team was out of town, she thought an awful lot about Charlie.

It was around three o'clock in the afternoon, the Wednesday the Seahawk's team returned. Loraine was at the beach, lying in a beach chair, warm breeze blowing across her smooth tanned skin.

"You know I have been thinking about you for two weeks now," Charlie said as he walked up beside Loraine, beach chair in hand. "You are looking mighty good there Loraine."

Loraine, startled a bit, lifted her head off the beach chair, raising her right hand to shield some of the sun's rays. As she looked in Charlie's direction squinting toward Charlie standing in the intense sunlight, she replied, "you're back early Charlie. I thought you guys were going to be back after 5. I was going to go over and meet you at the ballpark."

"We got away early this morning. All the guys were ready to get home. It's been a long two weeks," Charlie said as he unfolded the chair and took a seat next to Loraine.

"You're just in time Charlie," Loraine said as she reached for a tube of suntan lotion and handed it to Charlie. "Would you mind rubbing some lotion on my back?" she asked as she rolled over, exposing her bare back to the sun.

"I'd be happy to," Charlie replied as he took a seat on the edge of Loraine's chair and began massaging the lotion onto her back. "I can see you have been spending some time out here at the beach these past two weeks, Loraine. Your skin is so tanned now."

"It has been nice to have some time off. I heard the team played well while you guys were out of town. I saw where you won two more games. Doris told me you were having a great season."

"Yes, we played really well. The team is coming together. What have you been doing on your days off Loraine, besides hanging out here at the beach?" Charlie asked as he slowly massaged the lotion onto Loraine's back and shoulders.

"Not a lot. I went to lunch with Claire one day and we went shopping after. Had dinner with Doris and her daughters one night. I have been going into the office in the morning then trying to get out of there by lunch. Most of the afternoons I have spent out here in the sun. I could get used to this," Loraine said as she rolled over on her side, looking now in Charlie's direction.

"Like I was saying a few minutes ago Loraine, I thought about you often while I was gone. As a matter of fact, I imagined you lying here on the beach sunning yourself several times. It gets sort of lonely when you're traveling from place to place on a road trip," Charlie said as handed the tube of suntan lotion back to Loraine, now taking off his shirt and leaning back onto his beach chair.

"It's hard to imagine you being lonely for long Charlie," Loraine said sarcastically as she sat up and leaned forward rubbing some lotion on her long slender legs. "I thought you ball players had a girl in every town while you were on the road. I've seen how the women at the ballpark flock around you and the other players after the games."

"There are lots of pretty girls at the ballpark. The younger guys, they draw a lot of attention from the girls wherever we go," Charlie said as he stretched his arms up over his head toward the sun.

"You don't say," Loraine replied.

"Yes, there are always pretty women at the ballpark," Charlie replied deflecting the conversation away from the subject of other women. "But after being with you, none of those other girls could measure up. You set a high standard Loraine. It seems you have spoiled me for other women. I'm not sure exactly what to do about that."

Loraine was of course happy to hear this, although she hid her feelings as much as possible. But the truth was, Loraine had been thinking about Charlie for two solid weeks. She could not wait to get her hands on him as he laid out bare chested beside her. Truth was, whenever the two of them were together now, sparks flew. Charlie could not resist Loraine either, and she welcomed his advances. It was easy to see the attraction between them was mutual.

"You know Charlie, I have been out here for a couple of hours now and I need to get out of the sun. Maybe grab a bite to eat. You want to go grab a late lunch somewhere?"

"Yeah, that's fine with me," said Charlie.

"Let's go up to my condo and I'll hop in the shower and change into something else, and we can go," Loraine suggested as she stood up and began folding her chair.

Once they reached Loraine's condo, Charlie sat in the living room while Loraine went to shower and change. After a few minutes Loraine came out into the doorway of the room.

"Okay Charlie, I'm ready to go whenever you are," Loraine said standing behind Charlie.

Charlie turned to find Loraine standing there, wearing a red tank top, white gym shorts, flip flops and a Seahawks baseball cap.

"Loraine, if I didn't know better, I would think you were one of those college girls from Carolina working at the beach for the summer. This southern lifestyle is looking good on you," Charlie said as he stood up and walked over toward her. He wrapped his arms around her waist pulling her close to him.

"Well thank you Charlie," Loraine replied as she leaned forward and kissed him. "You know Charlie, I wasn't completely honest with you earlier. I thought about you a lot while you were gone. I missed you Charlie," she said as she kissed him again.

"I missed you too Loraine."

17

"Man am I glad to see you," Steve said as Bubba and Charlie walked through the lemonade company doors and into Steve's office. "It has been a crazy two weeks. The temporary delivery drivers we used while the players were out on the road, I don't think made a single delivery without causing a mess for somebody. Mostly me. Two of them didn't show up at all for work last week. And one that did show up for work backed into a car in the parking lot at the Dunes Club. It has been one thing after another since you have been gone Charlie."

"Well, at least I know you missed me," Charlie replied half laughing as he took a seat in a chair across from Steve's desk. Bubba lying on the floor next to his chair.

"I'm serious," Steve said exasperated by all that had gone wrong since Charlie and the Seahawk players had been out of town the past two weeks. Holding up a pile of paperwork from his desk, Steve continued, "things around here are a mess. We need to talk about this Charlie. This business is growing at such a fast pace, and we have so many new employees who don't know what they are doing. We need to find some people who can get something done around here. When you are gone, and I am here by myself I am overwhelmed. We need to seriously consider hiring some sharp, competent people who can help me run things when you are not here."

Charlie wasn't surprised to hear Steve's concerns. The lemonade business had grown so fast over the past two summers, that whenever Charlie was out of town on a road trip Steve would have these same types of problems. What had started as two guys selling frozen mixers out of a used van had grown into a large corporation.

"Hey, look Steve, you have done a great job with this business. I trust your judgement completely. If you think we need to hire some folks to help you run things when I am out of town, then by all means, start looking for some folks to help you run the business when I am away. I don't want all of this to fall on your shoulders. I will help all I can when I am here. But I am out of town basically half the summer when the team is on the road. I don't expect you to do this on your own while I am gone."

"I appreciate you saying you have faith in me Charlie, but these are big decisions, hiring the people we need to run this place. You and I, we both have a vested interest here. I don't want to make these types of decisions about who we hire unless we are both in agreement about these employees before I offer them a job. These are decisions that affect the both of us. I want you and I both to do the hiring and interviewing of these key people ourselves. I don't want to choose these key folks we need by myself."

"I understand Steve. I know all this work is falling on you and I don't want that. How many people do you think we need and where should we look to find these people?" Charlie asked.

"I think we need at least four supervisory people to handle managing the delivery drivers and the operations inside the building making and packaging the product. Then we need three fulltime outside sales reps to go into stores and hotels, and two sales reps to go into grocery stores and restaurants to make sure deliveries are happening properly and to solicit new accounts. In addition, I would like to have one key person inside the warehouse to manage all these new people. Someone who can run the day-to-day operations to make sure everything runs smoothly to take some of these day-to-day duties off our plates.

"We also need one key person to be out in the local community and another person traveling out of town to market the business. Since we started selling the Bubba's Frozen Lemonade hats and t-shirts with that new logo design we put on our trucks and packaging, we have orders coming in now from retail stores and several of the hotels wanting to sell them. We make a good margin on the hats and t-shirts, and we don't touch those. They go straight from the manufacturer to the stores, and we get a commission on all of those. They sold 300 t-shirts and 250 hats at the Seahawk's first home series at the ballpark.

"And lastly, we need an executive type person to be out in the public marketing the company brand. Someone who can represent our brand here in Myrtle Beach and call on our larger corporate contacts. That is going to be a key hire. It will take an experienced marketing rep with a proven track record to manage all that and represent our brand. That person will be hard to find and expensive to hire. But if we get the right person for that role, they will be a great help to us.

"We need these people Charlie, so you and I can go out and make business calls and meet with existing corporate clients and new potential customers. We need some help. The sooner we can find these people the better. I don't want to be choosing these people on my own. I want us to do this together. Once we get these people in place our lives will be a lot simpler."

"Alright then, it's settled," Charlie said as he leaned forward on the edge of his chair. "I'm sorry you have had to deal with all of this while I am gone Steve. I don't want you having to stress over all this work alone. I want to help you, to do my part. I agree with you 100%. You line up the interviews for the folks you want to hire, and I will be here, and we will talk with every one of these folks together. Then we will decide who we want in which positions. Just let me know when to be here and we will find the right folks for each of these positions."

"Great. I feel better already just knowing we will be getting these folks in place," Steve replied as he took a deep breath and leaned back in his chair trying to calm his frayed nerves.

"Hey, look Charlie," Steve said, trying to collect his thoughts after listing all the problems he had dealt with while Charlie was gone, "I haven't done a single thing but complain since you got here this morning buddy. Sorry about that man. It has been a long two weeks. I haven't asked you about your trip. I saw where you guys are in first place in the division, and you won two more games. You all are off to a fast start."

"Yeah, we are. The team is playing great. It was a good trip. Two weeks is a long time to be on the road. It's nice to be back. Look Steve, I do have something I would like to talk with you about. Something I have been thinking about for the last couple of weeks. I was wondering if I could come by your house tonight and we could talk. It concerns both you and Claire and I would rather not talk about it at the office."

"Is everything alright Charlie?" Steve asked.

"Yes, everything is fine. I have something I need to make a decision about, and I want to speak with you and Claire about it before I make up my mind. Are you going to be home tonight?"

"Yes, we will be home. Why don't you come over for dinner about 6:30 and once we eat and get the kids to bed the three of us can talk," Steve suggested.

"Perfect. I'll see you and Claire at 6:30."

18

"Claire, that roast was out of this world," Charlie said as he picked up his plate from the table and walked into the kitchen. "Thanks so much for having me over tonight."

"You're welcome, Charlie. I'm glad you liked it," Claire said as she took the plate from Charlie's hand and placed it in the sink. "Let me give you a slice of this pecan pie and then you and Steve go out on the back porch, and I will join y'all in a minute."

It was a beautiful summer night as Charlie and Steve sat out on the back porch of Steve's oceanfront home. The waves coming onshore a hundred yards or so in the distance, the sun just beginning to set, a warm breeze blowing from the south. Charlie had been to Steve and Claire's house many times. After all, they were the closest thing he had to family aside from his parents and brothers living in St Petersburg, Florida. Charlie valued Steve and Claire's friendship as well as their advice. He had spoken with them before on dinner visits regarding several other personal issues.

But tonight, was different. Tonight's conversation was about a subject that would affect all of them. Charlie was undecided what to do about the documentary. On the one hand he could see the value in sharing his story. But the last thing he wanted would be for his past to shine a negative light on Steve and his family. So, as he looked out toward the ocean, he was unsure where to begin. After about 30 minutes Claire had the kids in bed and joined Steve and Charlie on the porch.

"Charlie it is nice to have you over tonight, but I wish you would have brought Loraine to dinner with you." Claire continues, "she and I have become really good friends over these past few weeks. I really like her Charlie."

"Yeah, Loraine is great, and I do want us all to get together again sometime soon. But I had some personal business I wanted to speak with you and Steve about tonight."

"Sure, what is it you want to talk with us about Charlie?" Claire asked.

"You both know that a few weeks ago I was approached about doing a documentary with the Sports Channel and I told them I did not want to do it. But I have been thinking about that some more the past couple of weeks and I wanted to talk with you both about it before I decide."

"Well, I think it is a great idea," Steve said.

"I do too," Claire responded. "This would be a real honor for you Charlie, and if anyone is deserving of a documentary it is you."

"It is nice to be asked to do it," Charlie replied. "But I have some reservations about it and before I decide what to do, I wanted to talk with both of you because once we start filming the documentary it will be out of our control. I have dealt with the media before on a national level when I was playing ball in Chicago. A person's past is fair game once the press shines a light on you. And my past includes our relationship. I would not want to do a documentary on me and open the door for negative press to be written about Steve and myself. I don't want to hurt the business or your family, if I share details about my past struggles in a documentary.

"If I agree to do the documentary it will be hard for me to share some of the issues I know will come up about my past. I am still not sure if I want to put myself through all that. But I certainly would not want to do a documentary and it have a negative affect on the two of you. I wanted to talk with you about it. To see what your feelings are before I decide what to do."

"I appreciate your concern Charlie," Steve replied as he placed his plate of pecan pie on the coffee table next to his chair. "But I am not uncomfortable sharing my story. As a matter of fact, Claire and I have been discussing ways we can help more people. We have been so blessed. I am looking for ways to give back, like the Bubba Ball program. Think of how many kids and families that program has touched. We have been through some difficult things Charlie, you and I, but we are living proof that miracles can happen. Those are the kind of stories people need to hear."

"I agree Charlie," Claire replies, reaffirming Steve's thoughts on the matter. "Everyone struggles in this life, Charlie. I don't want to tell you what to do. I know this is a very personal decision, to put yourself out there this way. I have never been in the public eye the way you have so I would not want to say one way or the other what you should do. But as far as my feelings are concerned, I am proud of what you and Steve have overcome. And I am completely comfortable with you doing the documentary if that is what you want to do."

"What about the business, Steve?" Charlie continues, "what about your kids? People in your church and the community who know you, me, your family. If they start digging around about what I was doing all those years since I left Chicago, they will find some negative information that they might put in the documentary for the whole world to see. Is that something you would be comfortable with?"

"The way I see it Charlie, we are all parts of our past. You, me, everybody has a past. Some things we would like to change. But I am not ashamed of my past. I made some mistakes, you have made some mistakes, we all have. But look at where we were, and where we are now." Steve continues, "how could you describe where we came from to where we are now and not see that it was a miracle.

"I don't want to tell you what to do. This decision is up to you. But know this Charlie, you are the best friend I have ever had. You are like a brother to me. I would be honored to share my story and be a part of this documentary if you decide to do it."

Later that evening on his way home Charlie drove his Jeep over to Loraine's condominium. It was little past eleven by the time he arrived and called her cell phone.

"Loraine, I know it's late to be calling, but was wondering if I could come up and see you for a minute."

"Sure Charlie, come on up."

Once Charlie reached her apartment he and Loraine went and sat out on the covered patio facing the ocean.

"What's on your mind Charlie?" asked Loraine.

"I have been thinking about the documentary Loraine. If it's not too late, I would like to do it."

"That is great Charlie!" Loraine exclaimed. "That's wonderful news! I will call Herb Volkmann first thing in the morning. He asked me the last time I spoke with him if you had thought any more about it. I told him no, and that I wasn't going to ask you about it again. He will be excited to hear that you have changed you mind."

"Well, that's good. I am glad doing it is still an option."

"Wow, this is exciting Charlie! I have to ask you, what changed your mind about doing the documentary?"

"I have been thinking about doing the documentary for the past couple of weeks. There are some things it's time I talked about, so I can put the past behind me and move on."

19

The next six weeks passed quickly as the Seahawks continued their stellar play winning 21 of the next 30 games, while taking a three and one-half game lead on the second place Greenville Bulldogs.

Off the field the lemonade business was booming. During those six weeks Charlie and Steve hired five managerial employees and six full time experienced delivery drivers to help take some of the pressure off Steve.

Meanwhile, Loraine had called Herb Volkmann the morning after Charlie told her he would like to move forward with the documentary. So, on a Tuesday morning just three weeks before the all-star break, the Sports Channel crew arrived in Myrtle Beach to begin filming the documentary. The plan was to film footage of Charlie in game situations over the next three weeks and interview family and friends to get a personal, behind the scenes look into Charlie's life since leaving Chicago ten years earlier.

Over those six weeks Charlie and Loraine continued dating hot and heavy. There was no denying the chemistry developing between the two of them. Their relationship now was common knowledge with the staff working around the ballpark and the players and coaches in the dugout.

The combination of dating Loraine and making the decision to go forward with the documentary, seemed to have a calming effect on Charlie off and on the field. He was beginning to feel more and more like his old self again. On the field his workouts improved. He was throwing harder with less effort in his bullpen practices and in games. The velocity on his fastball increased and his control improved, now throwing his fastball consistently in the low 90-mph range over a seven inning start.

He was more focused. His self-confidence was returning. For the past eight years Charlie had battled insecurities about the health of his elbow. Never feeling completely comfortable with going 100% for fear of reinjuring it again. After all, it was the injury to his right elbow that took Charlie from the pinnacle of professional sports to a two-year rehabilitation hiatus from the game. During which time he could not throw a baseball from the pitcher's mound to home plate without pain.

Meanwhile, Herb Volkmann scheduled a scouting trip to Myrtle Beach the last two weeks of the filming. Back in Chicago the big team was playing playoff caliber baseball and Herb was looking to add some pieces to the big-league roster before the second half of the season. It was common knowledge that Romero, who had continued to pitch beautifully all season, would be leaving for Chicago at the mid-point of the season, along with power hitting third baseman Pete Roberts and right fielder Josh Harris.

It was a Friday morning just one day before the all-star break when the Sports Channel crew sat down for their final in-depth interview with Charlie. The next night the Sports Channel team would be filming game footage from Charlie's Saturday night start against the Jacksonville Bluefins.

"Charlie, you have been a busy man since you left Chicago ten years ago, still playing professional baseball and working with Bubba's Frozen Lemonade. You are having a great season, leading the league in ERA with a record of eight wins and only two losses on the season." Jeff Thomas the Sports Channel interviewer continued, "today, this will be our final interview for the documentary. There will be no questions. We want you to simply tell us your story, whatever you want to tell us about yourself. What you would want people to know about who you are, how you got here. Where you want to go and what your plans are for the future. We will just sit back and listen. Whenever you are ready to speak, begin. We will film for as long as you would like to talk. Whatever you want to tell us."

"First of all, I'd like to thank the Sports Channel for the opportunity to do this documentary," said Charlie. "It was not something I was planning on doing. But I am glad to be able to share my story."

Charlie continued, "ten years ago, when I left Chicago, I was a very different person than I am now. At that time baseball was my life. A 23-year-old kid, I felt invincible then. Sports had been the center of my life. I was so blessed. I had every opportunity come my way. Looking back on it now those things came so easy to me. I had great coaches and loving parents who supported me. I had teammates who helped me along the way to the big leagues. I was so fortunate. Being just a kid back then I took all that for granted. My health. The ability to play a game I loved for a living. It happened so fast I never really understood how lucky I was. Or that things could change so quickly.

"After my third season, when I had the elbow surgery and moved here to rehab my arm that summer, I went through a painful divorce. My arm was injured, and I developed a staph infection. During that time the pain in my arm was very intense. The infection caused swelling and stiffness to the point that I could not throw a baseball for two years. Suddenly everything in my life changed. I was alone a lot during those two years, and over time I became deeply depressed.

"It's not an easy thing to say about yourself, that I have been deeply depressed. But I need to say it so I can put it behind me. During those two years when I took the

105

prescription pain killers to ease the pain in my arm, I would drink to help settle my nerves. I never had a problem with alcohol before, but combining the alcohol with the pain medication took me to a deep, dark place. There were nights when I would be alone in my condo where the silence was so loud it was deafening. I began to believe my life would never get better. It was a dark and lonely place. I would not wish that on anyone.

"I grew up in a Christian home. My parents took us to church, and I believe in God. But when everything went wrong for me and the prescription drugs and the alcohol started to consume me, I began to lose my faith. I began to lose hope.

"I was in such a bad place, I felt I had nowhere to turn. Then when I felt there was no coming back from where I had fallen, a miracle happened. Steve Wilson and I had become very close friends over those two years. Steve and I were both battling similar demons. Steve had the strength to attend a rehab program at a local church. It was at one of those meetings where Steve met his now wife Claire Reynolds and her father Jack.

"It was there in that small church at a rehab meeting where Claire and Jack led Steve to Christ. Over the next six months Claire and Jack, and those people in that small church, loved on Steve and brought him out of addiction. It was a miracle.

"During that time, I watched the change in Steve. Like I said, I believed in God. I believed in miracles. But when I was so down, I lost hope that a miracle could happen for me. Watching Steve's transformation and the way Claire loved that man gave me hope that maybe, just maybe, if God could use Claire and Jack to save Steve, He could save me too.

"So, I began to attend weekly meetings with Steve. I got to know Claire and Jack. They never judged me. They just loved on me. They encouraged me to read my Bible again. I went to weekly Bible Studies. God gave me my health back. He gave me my mind back. He took away the desire for drugs and alcohol and replaced it with a desire to serve Him and know Him.

"As you know, at first, I did not want to do this documentary. I did not want to share my story. But after talking with Steve, Claire and Jack, I see that it is important for me to share my experiences. That people need to know that no matter where you find yourself in life, with Jesus there is always hope."

20

"Hey man. What are you doing here? Don't you have a ball game tonight?" Steve asked as Charlie and Bubba came walking into the lemonade company warehouse. "I didn't expect you to come into work today."

"I don't have to be at the ballpark until 5, the game is at 7. So, I had some time to kill. I thought we would swing by and see how things were going over here," Charlie said as he and Bubba walked into Steve's office and took a seat. Charlie in a chair across from Steve's desk and Bubba sprawling out on the floor beside him.

"Things are going really well today. The deliveries went out on schedule this morning which is great. The lemonade cart kids all showed up for work today which is by all accounts a minor miracle. And nothing crazy has happened that I know of. So, it has been a very good day around here so far," Steve said as he leaned back in his chair with a big smile on his face. "Where's Loraine? I thought you and her would be off somewhere doing something fun today on your day off. You should be out doing something with her instead of hanging out around here with me."

"I was planning on going to the beach with Loraine today," Charlie said as he leaned over to his right, looking away from Steve as he rubbed Bubba's head. "But it turns out Loraine had an unexpected meeting with Herb Volkmann at the stadium at 10 this morning. Herb told Loraine that she had done such a wonderful job here in Myrtle Beach this summer managing the stadium and working with the production crew from the Sports Channel, that they were going to announce that she would be going back to Chicago after the season ends and named National Sales Manager for the Chicago baseball organization's licensed products sales division. This is something she has worked hard for and wanted for a long time. The promotion will double her current salary. She was excited to get the news. It is a great opportunity for her."

"I see," Steve said, sensing that Charlie was upset by the news. "Loraine is a smart young woman. She will do a great job for them. I will be sorry to see her go. You know, she and Claire have become really good friends, and the kids love Loraine. They will all be sad to hear she will be leaving. So, I guess she will be here until the end of the baseball season and then leaving for good?"

"Yes, that's the deal," Charlie responded as he continued to pet Bubba, looking down toward the floor.

"I see," replied Steve.

Steve knew Charlie was upset. It was obvious. Charlie did not want Loraine to leave, he was crazy about her.

"Well, what are you going to do about this Charlie?" Steve asked. "You can't just let her go. You are already mopping around just knowing she will be leaving. You can't let her leave now. It's obvious you are crazy about her."

"I know. I am going to miss that girl." Charlie continues, "but really Steve, what can I say? Loraine, I want you to give up an opportunity you have worked so hard for? Something she told me she wanted and was working for from the first day I met her and has consistently worked so hard to achieve since she got here. I can't do that. I can't ask her to give up her dream."

"Charlie, I don't like to tell you what to do," Steve said as he leaned forward putting his elbows on his desk.

"Steve, you tell me what I should do all the time," Charlie said sarcastically looking down again toward Bubba lying on the floor next to him.

"Well, maybe I do. But still, man, you can't let Loraine go back to Chicago without telling her you are crazy for her. Charlie, there is nothing Loraine could have in Chicago she can't have here. She is a smart girl. If she wants a career, she can have that anywhere. Did you know the Sports Channel offered her a job? When they saw how competent and professional she was while working with them on the documentary, they offered her a job in their marketing division. Loraine will be successful at whatever she does. And there are lots of opportunities for someone like Loraine here in Myrtle Beach."

"Maybe so. But I can't ask her to choose between me and this opportunity. I have been in a long-distance relationship before, and you know how that turned out. I knew she would be leaving once the summer was over and she and I probably would not work out after that. But when I got the news today that she would be leaving for good once the season ends it bothered me more than I thought it would."

21

It was 4:45 pm when Charlie parked his Jeep in the players parking lot at Seahawk Stadium. Walking quietly into the clubhouse Charlie changed his clothes quickly and made his way out onto the outfield grass where he did some light stretching. Charlie had a lot on his mind as he prepared for tonight's game.

This would be the last game before the players had a seven-day break dividing the first and second half of the season. It would also be the last time Juan Romero, Pete Roberts and Josh Harris would be suiting up in a Seahawks uniform. The next time the three of them took the field they would be playing for the big team in Chicago's Belmont Park. Charlie was happy for his three teammates. They had worked hard for this opportunity. Just like Loraine, these three young players would be moving on to the pinnacle of their profession. To test their skills at the highest level, competing against the world's best players.

It was a bittersweet moment for Charlie. He had been to the top of the mountain in professional baseball. Charlie had been the starting pitcher in the All-Star game just ten years ago. He knew what it was like to take the mound, come face to face against the best baseball hitters on the planet and succeed. So, as he prepared for tonight's first pitch, he felt an anxious, almost angry sensation come over his body. He was edgy again. For the first time in a very long time, he felt like he had something to prove. To prove that he still had what it takes to compete and excel again at the highest level.

As Charlie was finishing his stretching routine and preparing to head over to the bullpen to warm up before tonight's game, Herb Volkmann came over to speak with Charlie.

"You know I stuck around tonight just so I could see you pitch one more time before heading back to Chicago," Herb said as he shook Charlie's hand. "You are having a great season, Charlie."

"Thanks Herb," Charlie replied as he grabbed his jacket and made his way toward the bullpen, the two of them now walking through the outfield grass.

"I am thinking we have an excellent chance to make the playoffs in Chicago this season," Herb said. "The team in Chicago is playing great baseball, and with the young players coming the second half of the season we will be in the playoff hunt all summer."

"I agree. They are playing playoff caliber baseball in Chicago. And these young guys are the real deal. They will be a great addition to the roster," Charlie replied.

"Well, you have a great game tonight, Charlie. I'll speak to you again after the ballgame," Herb said as he patted Charlie on the shoulder before turning to walk back toward the stadium concourse.

Thirty minutes later Charlie was standing on the first baseline with his teammates for the playing of the National Anthem. Herb now sitting in the stands right behind home plate next to the Seahawk's radar gun operator, charting pitches.

At 7:05 Charlie took to the mound and toed the rubber for his warmup pitches. Charlie was a naturally gifted athlete. He made everything look easy. His fluid delivery. Never appearing to be out of control. The baseball left his hand in a beautifully smooth motion. He never appeared to be throwing hard. The ball simply exploded when it left his hand. Ten years ago, when Charlie was the best pitcher in baseball, he made it all look so effortless. As Herb sat there behind home plate, watching Charlie deliver pitch after pitch with the same fluid motion he had seen when Charlie was a first-round draft choice right out of St. Petersburg High School, Herb wondered, *'how is this guy not pitching in the major leagues?'*

From the game's first pitch Charlie moved the ball around the plate. Fastballs, curve balls, sliders, changeups. Whatever pitch he wanted to throw came out of his hand in a fluid, effortless release. Painting the corners through six innings striking out ten while walking no one, giving up only two hits and no runs. His fastball topping out at 91 mph.

Then in the bottom of the sixth inning and the Seahawks leading 2-0, with a runner on first and two outs, Pete Roberts who was leading the Coastal League in homeruns came to the plate. With the count one ball and two strikes, Roberts hit a belt high fastball high into the Myrtle Beach sky, soaring over the left field bleachers giving the Seahawks a commanding 4 – 1 lead. After Roberts connected with the pitch, he flipped the bat up in the air before making his way around the bases. Robert's home run and flipping the bat gesture drew a spontaneous outburst from the Bluefins starting pitcher, the players and coaches in their dugout.

Right fielder Josh Harris was the next Seahawks batter. He dug his feet into the batter's box and took his stance. The Bluefins pitcher, still upset by Robert's homerun celebration, threw a 92-mph fastball high and inside striking Harris on his right cheekbone cutting a 3-inch laceration into Harris' face and knocking him to the ground unconscious. Immediately both benches emptied. A brawl ensued resulting in two Seahawks and three Bluefins players being ejected from the game. It was an ugly scene.

It was twenty minutes before the field could be cleared and play resumed. The next Seahawks batter hit a ground ball to second base for the third out of the inning.

Then in the bottom of the seventh inning Charlie took the mound for what typically would have been his last inning before giving way to the bullpen to finish the game. But as Charlie went to the mound, still fuming after seeing his teammate's bloody face, lying there on the ground unconscious, he was visibly shaken by what had happened. As he stood behind the mound glaring toward the Bluefins dugout, his anger rising inside of him, he forgot about being careful. He forgot about pacing himself. He forgot about protecting his arm. He was done with all that. He was angry. He was frustrated. It was time to turn that pent up energy loose. It was time to let it all go.

Charlie walked to the top of the mound. He took one more look toward the Bluefin dugout, glaring in their direction. The Bluefin players standing on the top of the dugout steps were still chattering their disapproval toward Charlie and the rest of the Seahawk players. After throwing his customary five warmup pitches, the first Bluefins batter stepped into the batter's box. Looking in toward the catcher behind home plate, focusing on his target, his eyes peering just above his glove, he went into his windup and delivered his first pitch of the inning, the ball exploding from his hand. Strike one. Herb Volkmann, sitting next to the radar gun operator looked over toward the flashing red light on the radar gun. 98-mph.

Eight pitches later Charlie walked off the mound taking a seat at the end of the Seahawk's dugout. No one in the dugout said a word to Charlie. After the inning was over instead of replacing Charlie with a reliever from the bullpen Charlie pitched both the eighth and ninth innings. Not a single Bluefin batter would reach first base over those two innings as Charlie retired all six batters he faced, striking out four Bluefin hitters while throwing just 18 pitches.

Immediately after the game as Charlie was walking with his teammates toward the Seahawk locker room beneath the stadium concourse Herb Volkmann met Charlie outside the locker room door.

"Charlie, I need to speak with you. You pitched a great game tonight, Charlie. You reminded me tonight of a young pitcher I used to watch pitch in Belmont Park. What happened out there tonight, Charlie?" Herb asked.

"I don't know. I have had a lot on my mind lately. And when Josh got hit in the sixth, I was so angry and upset seeing him lying there that way. I just got into a zone."

"A zone. Yeah, I would say you were in a zone alright, Charlie. You pitched a beautiful game. Major league caliber performance. Do you realize how hard you were throwing those last three innings? All your fastballs from the seventh through the ninth inning were over 97-mph and you threw three fastballs over 100-mph. We are off for the next seven days. Get your affairs here in Myrtle Beach in order. A week from tonight you will be pitching again in Chicago."

22

"Man, you brought the heat last night Charlie," Steve said shaking Charlie's hand as he and Charlie met at Flo's Diner the next morning for a quick breakfast before heading over to the warehouse to work out some business arrangements before Charlie's impending transfer to Chicago. "Then I saw on the Sports Channel after the game that you had thrown over 100-mph in the ninth inning and that you were going to be pitching in Chicago the rest of the season. Wow, that was amazing. That is so awesome Charlie. I am happy for you man!"

"Yeah, it's exciting. I was not expecting that to happen. Going back to Chicago was not something I dreamed I would experience again," Charlie responded as he and Steve took a seat and their waitress placed two orders of pancakes, sausage and eggs on their table. "I am thrilled to be going. But before I go Steve, I want to do all I can this week to help you get situated here. I don't want you to be shorthanded at work the rest of the summer while I am off playing baseball in Chicago.

"Those people we talked about you hiring to help you," Charlie said as he poured a hefty helping of syrup on his pancakes, "don't wait on hiring those people. I may not be here very often the next few months. I will either be playing in Chicago or on the road and I will not be able to be back to interview these folks with you. I don't want the business to suffer, or you here working day and night because I am not available. I want you to go ahead and hire these folks to help you. I know it's not an ideal situation with me being gone so much these next few months. So, go ahead and hire these folks to help you when you find them. I trust your judgement."

"Charlie, you just threw a 100-mph fastball. You are going to Chicago the end of the week. You finished the documentary and it will be airing in the next few days. You are the talk of the Sports Channel and professional baseball. The former Most Outstanding Player Award winner returns to the big leagues. And we are talking about hiring employees to work in the lemonade business? Come on man! I am so excited about all this! How can you be so calm Charlie?" Steve asked as he patted Charlie on the back. "Charlie I am so proud of you man!"

Over the next forty-five minutes as Charlie and Steve sat there in the diner eating their breakfast there was a steady stream of local people stopping by their table congratulating Charlie on his pitching performance the night before and wishing him good luck on his being called up to Chicago. Over the past ten years Charlie had become an important part of the Myrtle Beach community. He loved Myrtle Beach. It was home to him now. And while he was excited about playing baseball again at the highest level, he was sad to be leaving home.

After spending three years in the major leagues, Charlie understood that in professional sports, the same fans who will cheer for you one minute, will boo you the next. An athlete's value in professional sports is based on how you perform today. Charlie had lived away from the limelight long enough now to realize your true friends, your true fans, will be there in your corner when things are going well and when they are not. That was not something he understood before, when he was living the high life, living in the fast lane of the Chicago sports scene. So, while everyone today in this low country diner would be a Charlie Pace fan no matter what happened, he realized that going back to

Chicago, he would be going back into an entirely different arena. Where his approval rating among the fans in the Belmont Park stands would change minute by minute, pitch by pitch.

After breakfast Charlie and Steve spent the rest of the day at the lemonade warehouse going over the proposals from a few potential customers and working out some plans for expansion into new grocery stores and restaurants. Since the Food Chain expansion was announced, there were several other smaller grocery store groups and a few high-end restaurants in and around the Atlanta area that had approached Steve about selling Bubba's Frozen Lemonade in their stores. This would require additional delivery trucks and drivers to be hired to get the product delivered to these new customers.

"I think we should take advantage of these new opportunities Charlie," Steve said. "It's going to take a few additional trucks and employees to meet the demand. But it is a natural fit in this market if we do take on these new accounts. I think we need to do this. What do you think Charlie?"

"I agree, I think this is a good opportunity. But I am not going to be here to help you, Steve. Is this additional business something you want to handle now alone?"

"I am fine with it. Like I was telling you earlier, Jack told me he would help me run things while you are gone. And nobody understands business better than Jack."

"Okay, whatever you want to do about that go ahead and do it," Charlie responded.

"There is one more thing I want to talk with you about Charlie. I know you are going to be busy around town the rest of the week before you leave, and there is something we need to discuss before you go today."

"Sure Steve, what is it?" asked Charlie.

"I know we agreed when we first started this business that I would run things day to day, and you would help when you could, and that is fine. You also said you would like to keep your relationship with the business as private as possible while you were still playing baseball here in Myrtle Beach. But now that you are going to be playing in Chicago again, don't you think it would be a good idea to let our customers know, and potential customers know, that you are the majority stockholder in the lemonade business?" Steve asked. "Your name recognition as a professional athlete is what has opened the doors already to so many of the major accounts we now have. What do you think the impact would be on our business if we made it public that you are not just an employee of Bubba's Frozen Lemonade, you are a co-owner of the company? And besides, I have never felt I was honest with folks when they assume Claire and I own the company when really it is you and I who own Bubba's Frozen Lemonade."

"I don't know how I feel about that," Charlie replied.

"Look Charlie. I am not saying we must tell people. I am just suggesting we should think about it. Your ownership interest could be a huge asset to the company if we make it public. And these folks I am thinking about hiring, these key management people, they will want to know the make-up of the company ownership before committing to take the job. I can't lie to them and tell them I am the sole owner.

"Look at it this way Charlie. Our bankers know you are the majority owner. They know you put up the money to start the business. Our accountant knows you are an owner. There are some other people around town who have figured it out as well. Why hide it?"

"What people?" Charlie asked. "Who else knows?"

"Bubba's Frozen Lemonade? Come on Charlie. Bubba isn't my dog," Steve responded. "Why would I name my business after your dog? People have been asking me about the name of the company and who owned the business for years. There are several local people who have figured out that you and I own this business together. I have had lots of people who know both of us who have asked me why the lemonade business is named after your dog Charlie. I had someone who knows both of us ask me about that just recently."

"Who asked about that?" inquired Charlie.

"I'd rather not say," Steve replied. "Besides, I am thinking about hiring this person for one of these key management jobs we need to fill. I'll tell you who it is later if they take the job. Anyway, there are more people who know you own the company than you think already. So, I think with you going back to Chicago and the documentary being released in the next few days, it would be a good business decision if we were to let the public know you are more than just an employee here."

23

For the next four days Charlie was busy running about town, taking care of personal business and trying to help Steve as much as he could in the warehouse during the day while spending every minute he could with Loraine in the evenings after work. During Charlie's last few days before leaving for Chicago it was also decided that Bubba would spend the next few months with Steve and his family while Charlie was gone.

The news of Charlie's move to Chicago had taken Loraine by surprise. It came so unexpectantly she was not ready to process the reality that at the end of the week Charlie would be leaving. Anyone could see, Loraine was crazy about Charlie. Now, as she was just beginning to believe that the two of them may have a future together, Charlie was leaving. Even though they had only known each other for a few months, Loraine had fallen in love with Charlie. She wanted to tell him, but she was afraid. She was afraid that once Charlie left for Chicago their relationship might end. Loraine knew that once Charlie arrived in Chicago, he would be constantly surrounded by women looking to land the superstar athlete. That everywhere he went, to dinner, out to a bar, in a hotel lobby, traveling in airports and at the ballpark after games, Charlie would be approached by beautiful available women, while she was alone working in Myrtle Beach.

Loraine understood, having worked in the baseball organization, how many opportunities for relationships with other women there would be for Charlie once he left town. The thought of Charlie being in Chicago and playing on the road caused Loraine to doubt that their relationship could last. She was happy for Charlie. She loved him and wanted him to go, to follow his dream. But deep down inside, she was afraid. She was afraid she could lose him, and she didn't know what to do about it.

It was a little before 6:30, on a Thursday night, the night before Charlie was to leave for Chicago, when Charlie knocked on Loraine's condominium door. When Loraine answered the door, she was wearing her favorite black dress.

"Wow Loraine! You look so beautiful tonight. I love that dress," Charlie exclaimed as he leaned forward and kissed Loraine, a dozen red roses in hand. "I want to take you back to the marina for dinner tonight if that's alright with you?"

"Yes, that is fine with me. Thank you for the roses, Charlie. You didn't have to do that." Immediately Charlie could sense that Loraine was sad about him leaving. She hadn't been herself the past few days since getting the news. Since this was Charlie's last night in town, Loraine was trying to put on a brave face, but her eyes could not hide her heartache.

"I wanted you to have these roses, Loraine. I want tonight to be special. I'm glad you like them. Let's put them in some water and we will head out to dinner."

During the twenty-minute ride to the marina there was not much conversation between the two of them. Loraine looked out the window much of the way as Charlie tried to make small talk to lighten the mood. Once they reached the marina they went inside and sat at the same table they had dined at on their first date.

"I wanted to bring you back here tonight Loraine since this was where we ate on our first date. A lot has happened in these past three months," Charlie said as he pulled Loraine's chair out for her and she took her seat.

"Yes, it has," Loraine replied. "I want you to know how proud of you I am Charlie. I am not going to lie to you and say I am happy about you leaving tomorrow morning. I am happy for you though, and I will watch you play on television and keep up with how you and the team are doing. But I will miss you while you are gone."

"I will miss you too Loraine. I wanted to talk about a few things tonight before I go. I wanted to tell you again how happy I am for you and your promotion. You have worked hard for that promotion with the baseball organization. I know you have wanted it for a long time, and you have earned it. I think it's great and I am happy for you. But to be honest, I was disappointed when I heard the news you would be leaving Myrtle Beach at the end of the summer. I know that was your dream, but selfishly I wanted you to stay here and not go back to Chicago. I felt it was not my place to tell you it upset me when I first heard the news that you would be leaving, so I kept it to myself. But the idea of you leaving bothered me all the same.

"The first night we met Loraine, I told you that I wanted a family. To be married again someday and to have children, a family of my own. During these past several weeks since we have been dating, I have imagined what it would be like to have a family with you. There have been several times when we would be with Steve and Claire's children and I would see you with them, and I imagined what it would be like if those were our kids. If we were married with a family. Children of our own. Tell me Loraine, when you think about you and me, do you imagine us married with children one day? Is that something you see in your future?"

"I have thought about that. Yes, I have had some of those same feelings. I have wondered what it would be like to have a family with you too Charlie."

127

"You know I am leaving tomorrow morning Loraine and for the next few months, I will be either in Chicago or out traveling from town to town playing baseball. By the time the season is over you will be back in Chicago, and I will be back here in Myrtle Beach helping Steve with the business. So, there will not be much of an opportunity for us to be together during these next few months before you will be leaving for Chicago for good. Before I leave in the morning, I had to tell you, that I have fallen for you Loraine. I love you, and I don't want to lose you. There is something I need to ask you before I leave here tomorrow. Something I need to know before I go."

"What is it, Charlie?"

Charlie reached into his pocket and pulled out a small square box wrapped in red paper with a gold ribbon around it and placed it on the table, then he got down on one knee as he took Loraine's right hand in his.

"Loraine, will you marry me?"

24

"Welcome ladies and gentlemen to historic Belmont Park, this is Bill Thomas and Greg Wilson, on the WCGN Network, where tonight's nationally televised game between the Chicago baseball team, only two games out of first place in the Central Division behind their archrival St. Louis, will be playing host to the defending World Champion Nashville Knights. There has not been a night like this in Belmont Park since the team last won the pennant 32 years ago. There is excitement throughout the ballpark tonight because for the first time in many, many years Chicago is poised to make a playoff run in the second half of the season. But in addition to that, tonight will be the first time in ten years since Chicago's own, former Most Outstanding Player Award winner, Charlie Pace, will be taking the mound in a Chicago uniform. This game was sold out minutes after the announcement that Charlie Pace would be returning to the big leagues. As a matter of fact, since the announcement of Pace's return and with the team contending for the playoffs, all the team's remaining homes games have been sold out. You could not find an available ticket to tonight's game here in Chicago today at any price."

"That's right Bill, I have never seen excitement in Belmont Park like tonight. Tonight, marks the third game of a three games series between Chicago and the defending World Champion Knights. Chicago has won a game and lost a game in this series. A win tonight could move Chicago to just a game behind St. Louis. So, while tonight's game is critical in the playoff race, it is the return of Charlie Pace, a fan favorite in Chicago ten years ago that has captivated the baseball world. Not only here in Chicago, but the sports world nationally like nothing we have seen in a long, long time. Just this past Wednesday, the Sports Channel released an in-depth documentary where Pace discussed his injury and struggles with addictions and depression that ten years ago took him from the pinnacle of the sports world. The reaction to this documentary, and his miraculous return to the big leagues has touched the hearts of sports fans everywhere. When Pace takes the mound this evening, we expect an eruption of emotion from the sold-out Belmont Park fans fortunate enough to be here in attendance tonight."

Meanwhile, down in the Chicago bullpen Charlie was wrapping up his warmup pitches. His fluid delivery and pinpoint accuracy on display as the Chicago pitching coach stood by the mound admiring Charlie's immense talent as he went through his pregame warmup.

Then, just moments before the National Anthem was to be played, the announcement of the starting lineups was broadcast over the stadium loudspeakers. When Charlie's name was announced as the game's starting pitcher a crescendo erupted throughout the stadium. The emotion of the moment shook the usually unflappable Charlie. The noise was so loud and the outpouring of support so overwhelming, Charlie had to take a moment to collect himself. He tipped his cap to the fans hanging over the edge of the bleachers surrounding the bull pen. Then wiping a tear from his eye, he went back to work preparing for the game's first pitch.

At 7:05 Charlie walked from the first base dugout as the rest of the Chicago players raced out onto the field. When Charlie appeared across the top of the dugout steps and walked toward the pitcher's mound every person in the stadium came to their feet and together cheered with such a roar that the intensity of the applause reverberated across the Chicago skyline.

"Pace, Pace, Pace, Pace," screamed the fans in unison as Charlie took the mound and toed the pitching rubber preparing to begin his warmup, with his father, mother and new fiancé Loraine, sitting in the players box, directly behind the first base dugout. The noise was so loud and the ovation lasting for so long Charlie had to step back away from the pitcher's mound and acknowledge the fans ovation before he could quiet the crowd enough for the game to begin.

At exactly 7:15, a full ten minutes after the game's expected start time, Charlie stood atop the mound looking in toward the catcher waiting behind home plate for the game's first pitch, while his mind drifted away to a quiet, special place. A place where great athletes minds go when the noise and the emotion is so high there is simply no other way to block it out. Charlie's eyes visible just atop the baseball glove covering his left hand, he peered at his target and went into his windup. The baseball exploding from his right hand with such ease and grace, it appeared so effortless. The pitch accelerating toward the mitt, the hissing sound of a baseball traveling at over 100mph as it hit the catcher's mitt. Strike one. The radar gun in the centerfield grandstand registered 101mph.

Over the next seven innings Charlie pitched superbly. Giving up only two hits and walking no one while striking out 11 Nashville batters before being removed for a reliever in the eighth inning with Chicago leading 4-0. The team would go on to win the game 4-2 and move within one game of St. Louis in the race for the divisional championship.

After the game Charlie spoke to the media in the team's conference center.

"Charlie, what a performance tonight," said a Sports Channel reporter. "What was it like to be out there again on the mound tonight for the first time in ten years?"

"I don't know where to begin," Charlie answered. "It was amazing. I want to thank the fans for the way they came out and supported us tonight. The crowd was awesome. It means so much to the players to have the crowd behind us that way."

"Charlie, the Sports Channel documentary that was released this week," asked another reporter in the crowd, "where you shared your story, your battles since the injury to your arm. How has sharing those experiences and the outpouring of support you have received since the documentary aired affected your preparation for tonight's game? Would you say that after all you have experienced that your performance tonight is somewhat of a miracle?"

"I was nervous before tonight's game. No denying that. And the way the fans came out tonight and the ovation before the game, it was special. It was special because tonight I could feel the support of the fans. My family and my fiancée were here tonight. What a blessing to be able to be a part of a moment like that with them especially after the struggles I have had in the past. The injury to my arm, the staph infection. Then battling the addictions that followed was such a dark place. It's still hard to describe what it was like to be in a place like that.

"I went from the spotlight of being in professional baseball and doing what I loved one minute, to being in the darkest most dismal place you could imagine the next. From being a healthy young man living out the life I had dreamed about to being totally incapable of caring for myself physically, and emotionally. It was such a humbling existence. I would not wish that on anyone. But when I was at my lowest point, God sent people, many of whom I did not know before the injury, to support me. They helped me. They cared for me. When I had nothing to offer, they loved me anyway. They shared the love of Christ with me and brought me back to where I am sitting here tonight.

"Tonight, was great. It was an amazing experience. But I have seen miracles before. I know now that with Jesus in your life, anything is possible."

25

It was 8:00 am the following Tuesday as Loraine turned over in her bed and looked at the alarm clock on the nightstand beside her. It was the first morning she had slept in her own bed since leaving for Chicago with Charlie the morning after accepting Charlie's proposal of marriage. Loraine lay there quietly reflecting for a few minutes, as she looked around her bedroom. Then stretching her arms out above her, she sat up on the side of her bed. Her feet dangling off the bed, just inches above the floor beneath her. She thought about all that had happened the past ten days. It seemed like a dream; a dream come true.

Soon she was up and moving about. Changing into a pair of gym shorts, t-shirt and a Chicago baseball cap, autographed by her favorite major league player, Loraine laced up her tennis shoes. By 8:45 she was out the door, headed down the eleven flights of stairs and out into the hotel lobby and across the white sandy beach. She did some light stretching, then for the next 30 minutes she ran briskly down the beach.

By 10:20 Loraine was back in her condo. She grabbed some fruit and fixed a bowl of oatmeal with almonds. Grabbing a bottle of water from the refrigerator she walked out onto the balcony where she took a seat in a deck chair. Sitting quietly, she looked out across the expanse of ocean and sand beneath her.

Later at 11:45 Loraine parked her car in the Seahawk Stadium parking lot and made her way up to her office where she was scheduled to meet Doris and a potential new advertiser to discuss a business proposal. When Loraine entered the office suites Doris was waiting to greet her.

"Surprise!! Surprise!! Congratulations Loraine!!" rang out through the office suites and conference room as Loraine entered the room where Doris and all the office staff, along with Claire and some of her friends from Bible study were there waiting to surprise her. There was a table of Loraine's favorite southern foods: pulled pork barbecue, coleslaw, French fries, and hush puppies, along with a cake and sweet tea, waiting for her and the guests there to celebrate Loraine and Charlie's engagement. A large banner reading, "Congratulations Loraine," was hung across the wall.

"Oh my gosh," Loraine said laughing loudly as she smiled in surprise. "I was not expecting all this!! Doris, Claire, y'all shouldn't have done all this!! Doris, is this our 12am meeting crowd?"

"Yes, it is!!' Doris exclaimed as she walked over and put her arms around Loraine. "We all agreed we wanted to do something special for you Loraine!!"

"We are all so happy for you and Charlie!!" Claire echoed as she walked over and hugged Loraine. "Show us that ring girl!!" Claire continued, "tell us all about it, Loraine. Were you surprised when Charlie popped the question? Did you have any idea he was going to propose?"

"I can't lie. I have been hoping for this for a while," Loraine answered as she held out her left hand showing her new engagement ring to all the women in the room. Smiling from ear to ear at the oohs and aahs from the ladies in attendance as they examined her new ring. "But I was not expecting it. When he started getting all serious and talking about a family and kids at dinner, it got me hoping. But it happened so fast, I was shocked."

"Well, tell us Loraine, what happened next? So, you were at dinner when he asked you?" said Doris as she held Loraine's hand admiring the ring. "How did he ask you?"

"It was so romantic!" Loraine replied as the ladies in the room hung on her every word. "He took me to dinner at the restaurant where we went on our first date and told me he wanted to talk about a few things before he left for Chicago. The next thing I knew he pulled a box out of his pocket and placed it on the table. Then he got down on one knee and asked me to marry him!! It was amazing!! I have never been so happy!!" Loraine exclaimed as all the ladies roared their approval and congratulations.

"When did he tell you he was taking you to Chicago with him?" asked Claire.

"That night. He told me he wanted me to meet his parents and his brothers and their families. That his mom and dad would be at the game Saturday night, and he wanted me to go with him to Chicago and spend the week with his family. His mother and father are the nicest people. I met his brothers and their wives. His nieces and nephews were all at the game. It was wonderful."

"We were all watching the game at our house on TV Saturday night," Doris said. "When Charlie walked out of the dugout to the ovation from the crowd, oh my God! We were all there in our living room, Dave, me and the girls, cheering and crying. It was incredible to watch it on television. What was it like to be there in the stadium when that happened Loraine?"

"It was unbelievable," Loraine replied. "I have been to a lot of games in Belmont Park over the past seven years since I have been working for the baseball organization. But I have never seen anything like that. There was such an excitement in the stadium last week at every game with the team doing so well. But when Charlie walked out onto the field the stadium erupted. It was such a special moment to be there and see that.

"I knew Charlie was a fan favorite in Chicago. We still sold a lot of his jerseys in the sports merchandising department at the stadium and online," Loraine said, wiping the tears from her eyes, overcome with emotion as she described to the ladies in the room what happened next. "But I had no idea how popular a player he was and how highly regarded he was by the fans until being in Chicago with him last week. Everywhere we went people were stopping him asking for his autograph. Then Saturday when we got to the stadium before the game there were people everywhere in the stands and outside the ballpark wearing a Chicago, Charlie Pace baseball jersey number 27, with his name on the back. It was surreal to be there and see all that happening. Knowing that all this love and admiration was for someone you know. Then when he walked on the field, and again when he came out of the game after pitching at the end of the seventh inning the crowd noise was deafening. I will never forget that feeling for as long as I live."

After a few minutes of hugs and congratulations the ladies went through the buffet line and loaded their plates with the lunch organized by Doris and Claire. Then for the next hour or so the women talked about Loraine's trip to Chicago. The places she visited with Charlie and what his family was like. There were questions about wedding plans. Had a date been set? Where the two of them would live now that Charlie was back playing with the team in Chicago again? What was Loraine going to do after they got married? Was Loraine going back to Chicago after the season and work with the baseball merchandising department or would she stay in Myrtle Beach? So many things in Loraine's life were now up in the air. This engagement and Charlie's return to the major leagues was unexpected. And for the first time in a very long time, Loraine was truly excited about her future, with no idea where this new future may take her.

Later, after the guests began to leave the office, Loraine and Doris sat down in Loraine's office for a chat.

"Doris, I really appreciate you organizing all this for me today. You have been a great friend to me Doris. I can't thank you enough for everything you have done for me since I moved here this summer," said Loraine as she ate her second piece of cake.

"You're welcome, Loraine. And I am so, so happy for you and Charlie. Charlie is such a great guy. He is very shy and reserved when you first meet him. After all he has experienced it is easy to understand why he keeps his personal life so private. Watching the documentary that aired on the Sports Channel last week, when he talked about his struggles with addiction and how he recovered from that, I remembered how sad he was back then so vividly. How the church and Claire, Steve and Jack rescued him. I thought back to those years when he would come to the ballpark, and he was just a shell of himself. It was obvious to everyone that Charlie was hurting inside.

"It was as if he were dissolving before our eyes, and no one knew how to reach him. Then he started going to church and Bible studies with Steve. And later Jack, Steve and Claire started coming with him to the ballpark and sitting with him during games when Charlie was too weak to play. Them just being there for him when he was trying to rehabilitate his arm and get his confidence back. Charlie's problems, they kept that very quiet. It wasn't talked about in the dugout or in the offices. Herb Volkmann and the organization worked behind the scenes to make sure Charlie had the privacy he needed to recover. It was like a miracle to watch that documentary the other night and see where he is today, and how far he has come since his illness."

"It is a miracle," Loraine replied. "Charlie has told me a lot of things this week that he had not shared with me before about his battle with depression and addictions. I am not sure where this is leading him, but I do know he wants to find ways to share his story with more people. I know he and Steve are talking about beginning a Christian non-profit to help people in recovery. Since reading the Bible was so pivotal in their recovery, they want to go out into communities and begin Bible studies. Not just for addiction recovery, but for anyone who will attend a Bible study. Hoping that reading the Bible will lead more people to seek ways to serve people in need as they grow in their knowledge of Jesus' life and ministry.

"There is one other thing I wanted to speak with you about Doris," said Loraine.

"Sure Loraine. What is it?"

"As you know I will not be working here with the Seahawks in Myrtle Beach next year as the general manager. There will be someone else filling the general manager's position next year. I have spoken with Herb Volkmann about my replacement next season. I told him he would never find a better person to serve as general manager for the Seahawks than you Doris. He agreed.

"Doris, you have been such a blessing to me. Mr. Volkmann agreed, you have done a wonderful job here for many, many years. I asked Mr. Volkmann if I could be the one to tell you that you will be the new permanent general manager for the Seahawks beginning next season. Congratulations Doris!"

"Oh my gosh!!" exclaimed Doris as she reached out and hugged Loraine. "Are you serious Loraine? Really! I can't believe it!"

"Yes! Believe it Doris! I am so happy to be the one to tell you," Loraine said giving Doris a big congratulatory hug. "You will be the General Manager here next season. I know you will do a great job! You have earned it."

26

Over the next three weeks the Chicago team played championship caliber baseball. Going 11-4 over a 15-game stretch and taking a two and one-half game lead over the defending division champion St. Louis. During that stretch Charlie continued to pitch brilliantly winning his next three starts. Pushing his record to 4 wins and no loses with an ERA of just 2.39 while striking out an average of 11 batters per nine innings pitched.

Back in Myrtle Beach, Steve continued interviewing people for the management positions needed for the expanding lemonade business. He hired seven new people over the past four weeks since Charlie had left for Chicago. But he still had two key positions to fill. Steve had people in mind for those jobs, but he was waiting to speak to Charlie about a few details before making these last two hires.

It was Tuesday morning when Charlie made his way through the Chicago administration offices to an 11 am meeting with Chicago General Manager, Herb Volkmann. This was the first time Charlie had been in the administrative offices since returning to Chicago. A lot had changed in the administration department since Charlie played in Chicago ten years earlier. There were many new faces behind the administrative desks, as Charlie rode the elevators and walked through the building. For most of the people now working in the building, it was the first time they had seen Charlie in person. There were well-wishers all along the way, as Charlie met his admiring fans for the first time. There were people asking Charlie for autographs and selfie requests which Charlie happily agreed to as he walked to Mr.

Volkmann's office. As Charlie made his way to his morning meeting, he thought about all that had changed over the past month. It seemed like just yesterday, that Charlie was pitching in the minor leagues. Where many of the players on a minor league roster are playing professional baseball in relative obscurity. Mostly unknown names on the back of a jersey, random numbers on a scorecard, trying to make their way to the majors.

For Charlie, having been a former Most Outstanding Player Award Winner, while playing minor league baseball for the past ten years, he was asked for autographs occasionally at the ballpark, and always at business meetings when he traveled with Steve. But the return to Chicago and his success these past four weeks in the majors again, along with the airing of the Sports Center documentary, had suddenly put Charlie back in the center spotlight of professional baseball. Everywhere the team traveled on the road these past three weeks and around Chicago, Charlie was asked to sign autographs and pose for photographs. There were requests for speaking engagements and interviews several times a day, every day. Everywhere he went someone was asking something of Charlie.

But after his experiences in the past, specifically his sudden fall from grace after his elbow surgery, while Charlie appreciated the support of the fans, he understood that in the world of professional athletics, where the typical fan in the stands is concerned, you can go from the top of their list as a fan favorite to the bottom of the list very quickly.

"Charlie, come on in and have a seat," Herb said as he greeted Charlie with a handshake and pat on the back.

"Thank you, Herb. It's been a long time since I have been in your office. I think this is a new office isn't it, Herb?" Charlie asked as he looked around the room, with pictures of Herb and former Chicago players adorning the office walls. A picture of Herb and Charlie standing next to each other from the night Charlie won the league's Most Outstanding Player Award at the player's award banquet was displayed on the wall behind Herb's desk.

"Yes, it is Charlie. My office used to be down the hall. The organization did a remodeling of the building five years ago and moved me over here on the corner."

"I like it," Charlie said as he walked over toward a row of windows looking out onto the Belmont Park field.

"Yes, I do too. Have a seat, Charlie," Herb said as he motioned for Charlie to take a seat in one of the office chairs across from his desk. "Charlie, you have pitched great since coming back to Chicago. I am thrilled with your performance these past four weeks. I think we have a great chance to make the playoffs this year with the way the team is playing, and your contribution has been a large part of our success."

"Thank you, Herb. The team is playing great. The entire roster is contributing, and I am happy to be here to do my part," Charlie said as he sat down in a chair across from Herb's desk.

"How is your arm feeling Charlie? You look great. Your pitching has been super. And the velocity on your fastball has been consistently over 95-mph each of your seven inning outings since you arrived back here in Chicago. How is your recovery between starts? Are you having any issues with your elbow?" Herb asked.

"No, not at all. My arm feels great," Charlie replied. "The training staff has been super here, and I have learned a lot about taking care of my arm these past ten years since the elbow surgery. I do a lot of stretching now and I have a few exercises I do every day to keep my arm loose that I learned after my injury. So far, I have had little if any soreness the days after I pitch and I feel strong and ready to go on the days I am starting."

"That's great Charlie. So glad to hear that." Herb continued, "the reason I wanted to meet with you this morning Charlie, is I would like to talk some business with you. We have known each other for so long now, and this is just an informal meeting, so I wanted to speak with you myself without contacting your agent if that's okay with you. Then if you like we can set up a meeting with your agent to discuss details later if that's alright with you."

"That's fine with me Herb. What's on your mind?"

"Charlie, after speaking with the Chicago manager and pitching coaches, and reviewing the stats from your minor league season this spring before coming back to Chicago, we believe you are pitching as well as anyone in the majors. That you have some very productive years left in you as a major league pitcher and we want to offer you a long-term contract to pitch here in Chicago for the next five years. This would be a five-year commitment at $15 million dollars per season, guaranteed. We want to see you pitching in a Chicago uniform these next five years. You will be a free agent at the end of the season, and we know you may want to wait until the season ends to explore your options. But we want you to know we believe you are back Charlie. We believe you are healthy, and we like what we have seen from you, and we want to put our offer on the table. We want you to discuss this with your agent, and if you agree to the deal, we would like to formally sign you now and announce the deal within the next few weeks so you can concentrate on baseball. Knowing that your future here in Chicago is secure as we make our playoff run. How does that sound to you Charlie?"

"Wow," Charlie replied, "that is a wonderful offer, Herb. When I was drafted out of high school, I always wanted to begin and end my career here, in Chicago. This would be a dream come true for me Herb. I don't know what to say. Thank you."

"You're welcome, Charlie. If you will, talk to your agent as soon as you can, and we will work out the details."

"I will, thank you again Herb. Listen Herb, there is something I wanted to talk with you about before I leave if you have a few minutes?

"Sure Charlie, what is it?" Herb asked.

"Herb, I wanted to personally thank you for not giving up on me. We have never really talked about this before. But I wanted to thank you and the organization for sticking by me when I was having my problems. The way you and the team supported me and my family when I was recovering from the elbow surgery and kept my private life private while I was trying to recover from the depression and addictions that I was dealing with. I can't explain to you what that was like. But I wanted you to know, to hear it from me, how much your friendship and support meant to me."

"Charlie, you are welcome," Herb said as he fought back a tear trying to keep his composure. "I don't know what that was like for you Charlie, because I have not walked in your shoes. But I will tell you that the management team and the ownership of the ball club here in Chicago were very aware of the seriousness of what you were going through at that time. Everyone here in Chicago was heartbroken over your situation and were concerned for you and your family. We all know that professional baseball is a business. A huge, competitive business. But business should always be personal. And I can say that ownership, management, the coaching staff, we are all thrilled at your recovery and success. And on a personal note, I was very proud of you Charlie for doing the Sports Channel documentary and sharing your story. I was hoping when the Sports Channel approached us about the documentary that you would agree to do it and that would give you a platform to share your experiences. I hope you are happy with the way that turned out?"

"I am," Charlie responded. "I was not at all in favor of it, at first. Talking publicly about addiction and depression was not something I thought I would ever do. But I had a talk with my dad about it after my first start this season in Myrtle Beach and he told me the documentary might be a way for me to share my testimony and that we should be looking for ways as believers to witness whenever the opportunities present themselves. It was a hard decision to make. But I talked with Steve and Claire, and some people I trust in our church, and they agreed that by sharing our weaknesses we show God's strength. Especially when He leads us through circumstances we cannot handle on our own. I am not sure where God is leading me in all of this. I would have never thought at the beginning of the baseball season I would be sitting here with you today. But here I am. I am just trying to do my best day by day now. And I am excited to see where He leads me from here."

27

"Welcome ladies and gentlemen to Atlanta Stadium, where the Atlanta ball club will be playing host to visiting Chicago. This is Bill Thomas and Greg Wilson coming to you over WCGN Radio. Starting for Chicago on the mound for today's 1 pm ballgame will be Chicago former Most Outstanding Player Award winner, Charlie Pace. Pace has been the talk of professional baseball since making his return to the big leagues just 5 weeks ago. Over these past five weeks Pace is a perfect 5-0 in his five starts, with a league leading ERA of 2.37."

"That's right Bill, Pace is the talk of professional baseball and the sporting world. With Chicago now taking a solid three and one-half game lead on second place St. Louis with just five weeks remaining in the regular season, it appears that Chicago may snap it's dismal 14-year streak of not making the playoffs this season. In addition to Pace's outstanding pitching since returning to Chicago, rookie third baseman Pete Roberts and right fielder Josh Harris, along with veteran short stop Harold Davis and first baseman Ken Oliver, have been swinging hot bats for Chicago. There is the feeling in the air around Chicago and in the player's locker room that this team can make a deep run into the playoffs. All the pieces for a championship season appear to be in place. Now, its just a matter of wait and see as the teams sprint toward the end of the season, and hopefully for Chicago, a long overdue trip back to the playoffs."

It was a little before noon when Loraine parked her rental car in the Atlanta stadium parking lot. It had been three weeks since she had last seen Charlie. Chicago had been on the road for ten days at one point during these last three weeks, and the Seahawks were playing a home stand in Myrtle Beach the other days while Chicago was playing at home. So, with Loraine's job responsibilities and Charlie's travel schedule being what they were, this was the first weekend the two could meet.

By 12:30 Loraine had found her seat. She was sitting in a section reserved for Chicago player's wives and girlfriends. This was the first time Loraine had been to a road game sitting in the player's family seating section. She quickly introduced herself to the other wives and girlfriends, children and family members in attendance at the game. She was excited to meet everyone. As Charlie's fiancée, she was immediately welcomed into the group. And with Charlie playing so well and the team moving closer and closer to the playoffs, the ladies in the player's family section were all filled with excitement.

In the top of the first inning Chicago went three batters up - three down. Then in the bottom of the first when Charlie exited the dugout and walked toward the pitcher's mound, he received a standing ovation from the Atlanta crowd. This was the first time in ten years that Charlie pitched in Atlanta Stadium. His last appearance in Atlanta was when he was the starting pitcher for the National League in the Allstar game. As Charlie walked to the mound and the crowd rose to their feet a thunderous applause rang out across the stadium.

"Bill, we have been doing this a long time, but I have never seen ovations for a ballplayer like what we are seeing with Charlie Pace," said the WCGN Radio announcer.

"You are right Greg. His pitching has been spectacular since returning to the majors, there is no denying that. But it is his story of perseverance against all odds that I believe has captivated baseball fans and sports fans everywhere. Overcoming the injury to his arm and the staph infection that followed, the physical pain and rehabilitation with that plus his willingness to share openly his battles with addiction and depression. The human side of his story has touched the hearts of sports fans everywhere. In every stadium the Chicago team has played since Pace's return he has been greeted with a standing ovation. It is a tribute to Pace and a wonderful show of sportsmanship and appreciation by the fans."

Once the ovation ended Charlie toed the pitching rubber and went to work quickly dispatching the Atlanta hitters. Striking out two and retiring a third on a weak ground ball to first base, on just ten pitches. Over the next six innings Charlie was locked in a pitching duel with the Atlanta starting pitcher. Charlie moved the baseball around the plate with precision and accuracy. His fastball consistently above 95-mph, topping out at 101-mph. He struck out ten Atlanta batters while giving up only one run on four hits while walking no one. When Charlie was relieved in the eighth the game was tied one run apiece.

Chicago would score a run in the top of the ninth to take a 2-1 lead. But in the bottom of the ninth, Atlanta would score two runs to win the game 3-2. After the game Loraine met Charlie outside the players locker room with hugs and kisses that she had been saving just for him these past three weeks.

"Wow! That is my kind of hello, Loraine," Charlie said as he caught his breath. "Oh, my goodness, is that what married life is going to be like when I come home from being on the road? I could get used to a welcome like that," Charlie exclaimed as he squeezed Loraine tight in his powerful arms holding her athletic figure close to him now. "I missed you, Loraine. It is great to see you," he said as he kissed her again.

"You bet, big fella. This is how you are going to be treated whenever you come home. You can count on that," Loraine replied, as she hugged Charlie with all her might, resting her head against his chest. Then looking up toward him, she said, "I missed you too Charlie. I don't like this being apart for three weeks at a time. We have got to do something about this. I don't like you being gone so much."

"Me either," Charlie responded. "But the season won't last but a few weeks longer. Then we can make some plans, so we won't have to be apart so much of the time. This won't last forever. Look Loraine, I'm starved. Are you hungry? I need to get something to eat."

"I ate a hot dog during the game, but I could stand to eat something too," Loraine replied as she took Charlie by the hand.

"Let's go ahead and get going then," responded Charlie. "I do need to eat and there is something I want to tell you over dinner."

Soon Loraine and Charlie were in her rental car, headed to get something for dinner. Once they arrived at the restaurant, while waiting in the lobby for a table several of the other restaurant guests and waiters and waitresses recognized Charlie. He was soon being asked for autographs and photos which he obligingly agreed to. After about fifteen minutes a table was available, and Loraine and Charlie took a seat.

"Do you ever get tired of that? People asking for autographs and posing for pictures?" Loraine asked.

"Sometimes it gets a little overwhelming. Trying to say yes when I am tired and just want some privacy. But it is part of the job. Without the fans, we would not have the opportunities we have as ballplayers. When I was younger before getting to the big leagues, if I had seen a player on a team I followed, I would have asked him for an autograph or a picture. So, I am happy to do it. I appreciate the fans."

For the next forty-five minutes or so Charlie ate his food while Loraine filled him in on all that had happened in Myrtle Beach over the past three weeks. She told him about her surprise engagement party given by Doris and Claire. How surprised she was and how much she appreciated all they had done for her. She told Charlie that Doris had been named the new General Manager for the Seahawks and how excited Doris was to have this new opportunity.

Loraine shared with Charlie that she had been talking with Claire about wedding plans and how, if it was okay with him, she preferred a small private ceremony with family and a few friends at their church in Myrtle Beach as soon as the season was over. Loraine talked about how she had asked Claire and Doris to be her co-matrons of honor and the three of them were making plans to go shopping for wedding dresses and bridesmaid dresses soon. She also wanted Claire and Steve's children to be the ring barrier and flower girl at their wedding.

Then after the wedding they could have a reception at the Marina where they went on their first date. Loraine said she even had some ideas about places for their honeymoon. Charlie smiled and told Loraine that as long as the two of them would be going together, wherever she wanted to go on their honeymoon would be fine with him.

Finally, after Loraine had said all that, she asked, "Well Charlie, what is new with you? What have you been doing besides playing baseball these last three weeks?"

"Well Loraine, I did have one exciting thing happen this past Tuesday. I met with Herb Volkmann that morning, and he told me the Chicago organization and the coaching staff were happy with the way I have been playing this season and they wanted to sign me to a five-year $15 million dollar a year contract. My agent said he has had several inquiries already from other teams about signing me after the season is over since I will be a free agent then and we might could get an even higher offer. But I would like to begin and finish my career in Chicago. What do you think I should do Loraine?"

Loraine's jaw dropped wide open as she reached out and grabbed Charlie's right hand. "Oh my God Charlie! Did you say $15 million dollars a year for five years?"

"Yep."

"$15 million dollars a year for five years?"

"Yep."

"What do you do with $15 million dollars a year for five years Charlie?" Loraine asked as she started to smile and giggle out loud still squeezing Charlie's hand.

"I'm sure we will think of something," Charlie chuckled. "So, do you think this is a good deal? Do you think we should take this deal Loraine? My agent has all the details worked out and I am ready to sign, but since we will be married soon, I wanted to talk to you and get your approval before I signed."

Loraine got up out of her chair and walked over to where Charlie was sitting and sat down in Charlie's lap. She wrapped her arms around him and kissed him. "I am so proud of you Charlie Pace. Whatever you want is what I want. Is this what you want Charlie?"

"Yes, it is."

"Then take the deal Charlie."

28

"Steve, man, it's good to see you," Charlie said reaching out to shake Steve's hand as Steve exited through the passenger gate at the Chicago International Airport.

"Yeah Charlie, it's great to see you too," Steve replied as he gave his close friend Charlie a hug. "It's hard to believe it's been six weeks since you were last in Myrtle Beach. Everyone at the lemonade company is super excited for you," Steve exclaimed as he and Charlie walked toward the baggage claim escalator. While waiting for Steve's bags to come down the baggage line, within minutes Charlie was swarmed over by adoring fans asking for his autograph and posing for pictures.

"I appreciate you coming to pick me up Charlie. It's not every day I have a superstar major league pitcher give me a ride from the airport with people flocking all around us. I feel like I am somebody special to be getting all this attention," laughed Steve.

Over the next twenty minutes or so Charlie signed a couple of dozen autographs and posed for even more pictures. Then once Steve's luggage was retrieved, Steve and Charlie made their way through the airport and out to the parking lot. They then took a taxi to Loraine's apartment where Charlie had been living since coming to Chicago. They got Steve's luggage settled in the apartment's spare bedroom, then the two of them headed over to Belmont Park for the team's Friday night game against their division rival St. Louis. Juan Romero, Charlie's rookie teammate from Myrtle Beach, would be the starting pitcher for the Friday night game with a 7pm start time. This would be the first game of a three-game home series with St. Louis. With Chicago now holding a commanding five game lead on St. Louis with only 18 games to be played over the next three weeks to complete the regular season. Charlie was scheduled to pitch the Saturday afternoon game the next day.

Once they arrived at the ballpark Charlie took Steve down below the stadium concourse, into the player's locker room where he introduced Steve to his teammates. Then once the game began Steve sat in the team box with Herb Volkmann.

From the first inning on, Chicago's Romero pitched beautifully. This was Romero's sixth start in the big leagues. Over his first five starts he had a solid 2-2 record, his ERA was a respectable 3.97 as a starter, and he had made three appearances out of the bullpen as well. With the addition of Charlie to the starting rotation, Chicago had four solid starting pitchers not including Romero. So, the coaching staff tried to get Romero the innings he needed to stay sharp and use him out of the bullpen as a potential late innings closer. They wanted to use Romero in ways to best help the ball club, as they prepared for the playoffs.

With Romero pitching well and the team playing good defense behind him, Chicago jumped out to a 7-3 lead through six innings before Romero was replaced by a middle reliever in the seventh inning. The team would go on to win the game 8-5, taking an almost insurmountable six game lead over St. Louis with only 17 games left in the regular season.

After the game, Steve and Charlie grabbed a late dinner at a downtown restaurant near the stadium. Then they took a taxi back to Loraine's apartment. The next morning Charlie was up early and out to the ballpark by 10am to prepare for the noon time ballgame.

As Charlie loosened up in the bullpen before the game, he felt a little soreness in his right shoulder. Not anything to be concerned about. Just some stiffness, the kind of aches and pains athletes have from time to time during a grueling season in professional baseball. 162 games over a five and ½ month period is an awful lot of baseball. Between his first half of the season in Myrtle Beach and the time he had spent in Chicago, this would be his 17th start of the season. So, as he went through his stretching routine and later his warmup pitches Charlie focused on his control and limited the speed on his fastball to protect his arm.

It was a warm breezy day at Belmont Park, temperature over 90 degrees when Charlie took the mound at 12:05 pm. With the sold-out crowd standing and roaring around him, Charlie stood atop the pitching rubber looking in toward home plate. Nine pitches later Charlie had struck out three St. Louis batters. Charlie calmly walked in from the mound toward the Chicago dugout, the Belmont Park stadium on its feet.

Over the next six innings Charlie struck out seven more St. Louis batters, allowing no-hits and walking no one. Mixing up his pitches, curves, sliders, changeups, changing speed on his fastball, from 90 to 100-mph at will. Charlie's command of the pitches and the pinpoint precision of his throws were simply more than the St. Louis hitters could adjust to as the game wore on. With Charlie pitching a perfect game through seven innings, instead of bringing in a reliever, it was decided that Charlie would continue pitching into the eighth.

Charlie got the next three St. Louis hitters out in order. The perfect game now going into the ninth inning. Three outs to go for a perfect game. Then with one out in the ninth and Charlie's pitch count at 115 pitches, St. Louis all-star 3rd baseman Fredrick Lopez hit a knee-high slider into

157

the left field bleachers, breaking up the perfect game. After Lopez's home run the Chicago manager came out onto the mound and replaced Charlie with a pitcher from the Chicago bullpen. As Charlie exited the mound, he received yet another standing ovation from the Belmont Park crowd. Chicago would go on to win the game 4-1 taking a seven-game lead over St. Louis.

After the game Charlie and Steve took a taxi back over to Loraine's apartment. Soon after their arrival they had two large rib eye steaks cooking on the grill as they sat relaxed on Loraine's back yard patio.

"That was some game today, Charlie," Steve said as he stood next to the charcoal grill, sprinkling a hefty portion of seasoning on the two steaks. "That crowd noise was deafening when you were out there pitching. It sounded like the helicopters back at Fort Bragg when I was in the army. You look so calm out there. With all that noise, how do you do it?"

"You just get used to it after a while. I don't know how else to explain it," Charlie said as he leaned back in a deck chair, cold beer in his hand. "When I first came to the big leagues years ago, that was the biggest adjustment for me. The crowd noise and the size of the stadiums. You really can't explain what that is like to someone unless you have been out there and experienced it. It is an issue for a lot of rookies, the change in the crowd noise and the stadium size, the number of people at the games. Nothing really prepares you for that. You just have to get used to it if you are going to last in the big leagues."

Over the next two hours Steve and Charlie talked. Talked about all the things two guys talk about when they haven't seen each other for a while. They talked about Steve's family. How the kids were doing. How Claire and Loraine were working on arrangements for the wedding.

What was going on at work with Steve and the Lemonade business, how each of their golf games were. Charlie was not putting well, and Steve was having trouble hitting his driver in the fairway. Where and when they were going to plan their next golf trip with Charlie's dad and Jack once the season ended. And about Charlie's new contract with Chicago and what that would mean for Charlie, Loraine, and Charlie's ability to help Steve out with the Lemonade business.

"Charlie, have you thought about where you and Loraine will live once the season is over? Man, I am so happy for you guys, and the new contract, five years playing here in Chicago. That is a dream come true for you I know. Have you had much time to think about where you want to be during the season and the off season? What your plans are now that you will be playing in the majors again for at least five more years?" Steve asked.

"I have. I am thinking we will live in Myrtle Beach year-round and we will keep this apartment here for a while anyway. Loraine loves Myrtle Beach. She is crazy about Claire and Doris and the girls in her Bible study. I think she loves Myrtle Beach as much as I do now."

"Have you talked to her about her job?" Steve asked. "Is she still planning on coming back to Chicago after the season ends and working with the baseball organization here? Has she decided what she wants to do about that?"

"I am not sure what she wants to do about her job. She hasn't said anything to me about that one way or the other," Charlie replied.

"Well look Charlie. I have an idea I want to run by you."

"Okay, what is it?" Charlie asked as he got a second beer from the cooler.

"I have been thinking about the business and you being committed to the team here in Chicago for the next five years. I know you will be limited in what you can do with our business day to day because of your commitments here and I completely understand that. So, I was thinking, we need someone to represent the company. Someone who will care about it as much as we do. Someone we can trust. Someone we want to represent us and the company wherever they go. Someone who is professional. Someone who knows how to get things done.

"Charlie, what would you think about us hiring Loraine?

"We could let her make her own schedule. She can travel with you on the road and make contacts throughout the baseball season. Then during the off-season, she can be in Myrtle Beach with you and work from there. She would be perfect for us Charlie. What do you think?"

"I think that would be great if she wants to do it. But I don't want to make that decision for her. And I sort of hate to be the one to ask her about it. I don't want to pressure her into making a decision about her job, Steve. After all, we aren't even married yet," Charlie replied as he leaned back and thought about it. Him and Loraine being married and working together and all the complications that might cause. Charlie knew, it's not always easy for two married people to work together. He took a long sip on his cold beer, and he imagined what that might be like. Charlie quickly realized that with Loraine's perfectionist personality and how driven she was and him being so easy going, if Loraine went to work with the Lemonade Company, Charlie would soon be working for Loraine!

"Well, she isn't exactly working for us. She is going to be married to you and that makes her a co-owner. She would really be working for herself. Don't you think?" said Steve.

"I guess so, sort of," Charlie replied.

"She does know you are a part owner of Bubba's Frozen Lemonade, doesn't she? You have told her? Right, Charlie?"

"Well, not exactly."

"You asked the woman to marry you, and you haven't told her you own half the business?"

"Not exactly."

29

Over the next several days while they were together in Chicago, before Steve headed back to Myrtle Beach, Charlie and Steve had several conversations about Loraine working in the lemonade business. It was decided that if Steve felt Loraine working for Bubba's Frozen Lemonade was the best thing for the company, that he should ask Loraine about it and see what she wanted to do. Charlie told Steve he did not want to be involved in that decision one way or the other. The last thing Charlie wanted was to marry Loraine and then also be her boss. He knew that would not be good.

So, Charlie told Steve he would tell Loraine that Steve had an opportunity with the lemonade company he wanted to talk with her about, and that whatever she decided about her job was fine with him.

It was on a Monday morning the following week at 10am when Loraine met Steve to talk about this new opportunity.

"Loraine, thanks for coming over this morning," Steve said as he welcomed Loraine into his office. She was as usual very professionally dressed for their meeting. Loraine had an idea what Steve was going to speak with her about. Charlie told Loraine there was a position they needed to fill at the Lemonade Company and that he thought Loraine would be a good fit for the job. But Charlie did not give her any specifics.

"Well thanks for having me over Steve," Loraine responded as she took her seat. "Charlie has told me very little about this new opportunity with the company. But I love your product line. And since Charlie and you have been working on this business together for so long now, I am flattered you guys are considering me to be a part of the company."

When Charlie and Steve last talked, Charlie never did tell Steve if he told Loraine he was a co-owner of the business, instead of him simply working for Steve. So, as Steve began the conversation, he did not know whether to tell Loraine, Charlie was a co-owner or not?

"Well, yes Loraine. I, we, are very excited about the possibility of you becoming involved in the company. After all, Charlie and I have been working on this company from the beginning. It's as if it is both our baby, since we began it together."

"I understand how it would feel that way. When you are there at the beginning of something, whether you are an owner, or just an employee, it is special," said Loraine.

"Yes, yes, it is," Steve replied as he thought to himself, *'I have no idea how to bring this ownership thing up. Dag gone Charlie; you have made a mess for me boy.'*

"Well, let me tell you about the opportunity we have here Loraine, and you think about if it is a good fit for you. You don't have to decide right away. You can take some time and think about it." Steve continues, "we have been very blessed to have Bubba's Frozen Lemonade increase sales by nearly 50% over the past year with an expansion into the Food Chain in Atlanta and by picking up some smaller restaurant chains and grocery stores in and around the Atlanta area. With the contacts we have already, and the exposure we have with Charlie's recent success returning to the major leagues, we feel we have even greater possibilities to expand the business.

"Before Charlie went back to Chicago, we had decided to hire a National Marketing Director. The role of this person would be to help us make contacts with new customers and visit our current customers to solidify accounts and open new accounts as well. That was something Charlie and I were doing together before. Between me working in the business every day already, and Charlie playing baseball we could barely keep up. Now that he is going to be in Chicago half the year for at least the next five years, this new position is even more important for the business.

"I have been thinking for some time that you would be a perfect fit for this new position. And now that you and Charlie are going to be married soon, and with his affiliation with the company, I, we, wanted to offer the position to you, if it is something you would be interested in. We don't want you to feel any pressure to take the job. But if you did want to do it, we think you would be great at it."

"Steve, I think I would be interested. Tell me, what about a salary? And my work schedule?" Loraine asked.

"I, we, would be willing to pay you whatever you would be making in your new job in Chicago plus a 25% pay increase. And there would be additional bonus opportunities depending on sales increases from year to year. We also have a profit-sharing plan you would be a part of and of course we have health care and maternity benefits. As far as schedule goes, you will be working here in Myrtle Beach and making calls on the road as well. You could live and work in Chicago during the baseball season and work remotely if you like. The schedule is pretty flexible, since your role will be making contacts with customers. You could in essence work from anywhere anytime when the opportunity arises to meet with a client. On the phone, emails, face to face visits. What we need is for this new person to be the face of the franchise so to speak."

"Well, that sounds great to me Steve. That sounds like something I would really enjoy doing. When would I start?" asked Loraine.

"Anytime. The sooner the better."

"How about the first of next month. I would need to give Mr. Volkmann a 30-day notice so he can find a replacement for me in Chicago."

"That's great Loraine. So, excited to have you as a part of the business."

"Thank you, Steve," said Loraine as she stood up and shook Steve's hand then she turned and walked out the office door.

As soon as Loraine left, Steve called Charlie on his cell phone.

"Hey man, how did it go?" Charlie asked.

"It went great. She was super excited, and she took the job!" exclaimed Steve.

"What did she say when you told her I owned half the Lemonade Company?" Charlie asked expectantly.

"That didn't come up."

"What? Didn't you tell her?!" asked Charlie rather loudly.

"Not exactly."

30

"Ladies and Gentlemen, this is Bill Thomas and Greg Wilson coming to you live from St. Louis Municipal Stadium, where tonight the Chicago baseball team will be attempting to clinch the Midwestern Divisional Championship. With Chicago holding an eight-game lead with only nine games to play over second place St. Louis, a win tonight would clinch the division for Chicago. On the mound tonight for Chicago will be former Most Outstanding Player Award Winner, Charlie Pace. Pace, who has a 9-0 record will be seeking his tenth consecutive win of the season tonight when he takes the mound for our 6:05 start time. Pace is averaging ten strikeouts against only two walks per nine innings pitched, with a league leading ERA of just 2.08. And the talk in the media outlets across the country is that Pace appears to be a shoe in for this year's Comeback Player of the Year Award in professional baseball."

It was 5:30 as Charlie went through his stretching routine in the visitor's bullpen preparing for his pregame warmup. As he stretched out his back, legs, arms and shoulders he noticed there was more stiffness in his right shoulder and elbow than in his previous start. The temperature in the low 90's helped Charlie loosen his sore muscles, but still there was a noticeable amount of discomfort in his right arm as he went through his warm-up pitches.

In the top of the first inning Chicago came out of the gate swinging the bats scoring three runs in the top of the first inning. Then in the bottom of the first when Charlie took the mound, the stiffness in Charlie's arm and elbow improved. He would go on to pitch six solid innings, striking out eight St. Louis batters and walking two, while giving up four hits before being removed with Chicago leading by a score of 5-2. In the bottom of the seventh Juan Romero came on in relief and pitched three shutout innings giving Chicago the win and clinching the division as Charlie improved his record to 10-0. After the game Charlie spoke to the reporters in the St. Louis media center.

"Charlie, congratulations on another solid pitching performance tonight," commented one of the sportswriters in the press core. "What was it like to be on the mound tonight pitching with a divisional championship on the line and locking up a playoff spot for Chicago?"

"It was an awesome experience tonight," Charlie replied. "The team has played well all year. The guys in the locker room and management, the coaching staff. Everyone has done their job all season and I am very thankful to be a part of it."

"Romero had another strong outing in relief tonight," said a Sports Channel reporter in attendance. "Do you think he will be used coming out of the bullpen the rest of the season?"

"I don't make those decisions," Charlie replied as he drank a sip of bottled water. "But he has done extremely well coming out of the bullpen when called upon. That is a very difficult role, to come out of the bullpen in the middle of a close ball game and pitch at a high level. I have only pitched in relief a few times in my career. It was not an easy thing to do. But Romero is a very talented young pitcher. He has a calm demeanor and a very bright future in professional baseball. We are lucky to have him on our pitching staff here in Chicago."

"Charlie, the season began for you in Myrtle Beach, ten years removed from your Most Outstanding Player

Award season. Now you are sitting here in St. Louis, after pitching the winning game as Chicago clinches the division for the first time in over 15 years. What has it been like for you this season on a personal level to be a part of all that?" asked a syndicated columnist from a national paper.

"It has been a wonderful ride. To be sitting in here with you guys talking about Chicago winning the division and me being a part of that. Never in my wildest dreams would I have seen this scenario playing out back in March and early April as I was getting ready for the start of the season.

"I have played in the big leagues and had success at this level of baseball before. So, I am not surprised that I could still compete at this level physically. But after all that has happened these past ten years, I was not sure I still had the desire to play in the big leagues again. I did not trust my arm 100%. There is also a tremendous amount of scrutiny on a person who is a professional athlete. I was not sure I wanted to go back into that type of environment again. It can be like living in a fishbowl sometimes, with so many people watching how you play on the field and what you do with your life off the field. Honestly, I think the fear of being examined by the press and the sports fans kept me from really pushing myself to get back here to the majors.

"But I am in a very good place in my life now. I am engaged to a wonderful woman, and I have a great family who love me and support me no matter what. The organization here in Chicago, Herb Volkmann the General Manager and the ownership, the coaching staff. They have put together a great team and they support us 100%, and it is showing by the way the team is performing on the field. I feel blessed to be here, and I am excited to see how this team will do once the playoffs begin in a couple of weeks."

31

"Bubba, wow boy! It is good to see you boy!" Charlie shouted as he knelt on one knee and wrapped his arms around Bubba's neck. Bubba was wagging his tail so hard his whole body was shaking as he licked Charlie's face. "I know, I know, I missed you too," Charlie responded with a huge smile on his face.

With the team winning the division and clinching a playoff berth Charlie took a couple of personal leave days and flew back to Myrtle Beach before his next start. It was the first time Charlie had been back to Myrtle Beach since leaving for Chicago.

"Good to have you back in town," Steve said as he gave Charlie a handshake and a hug. "Looks like Bubba is mighty happy you are going to be home for a few days. He has sort of moped around our house since you have been gone."

"It is great to be back. When I got in my Jeep and drove over here to the warehouse this morning it seemed like a dream," Charlie replied as he continued to lean over, now rubbing Bubba's head and back with his right hand. "I sure have missed seeing everyone. And this old dog of mine. I have missed having him around that's for sure.

"I can see we have some more people working around here now Steve. And wow, those are some nice delivery trucks, this place is rocking."

"We are super busy now," Steve replied as he, Charlie and Bubba, whose tail was still wagging almost uncontrollably, made their way through the warehouse stopping every few feet as Charlie shook the hands and hugged many of the lemonade company employees, he had not seen in a couple of months now. There were lemonade cart vendors, delivery drivers, lemonade production workers scattered across the warehouse preparing for the day's deliveries. Many of whom were meeting Charlie for the first time. After about 30 minutes of handshakes and hugs Charlie, Steve and Bubba made their way to Steve's office where Steve took a seat behind his desk and Charlie sat in a chair across from him. Bubba now taking his usual position sprawled out on the floor beside Charlie's chair.

"So how are things going now that you have some more help around here Steve?"

"Things are going well. Our work schedule is running much smoother now that we have some experienced drivers. And the lemonade cart vendors, the part time kids, they are doing a much better job now that they have been working for a few weeks and have gotten into a routine. Business is booming. So that is a good thing."

"That's great," Charlie replied. "Are you more relaxed now Steve? Now that we have some people in place to help you out."

"Yes and no," Steve replied.

"Yes, and no? What do you mean yes and no?"

"Things are running smoother with the new people for sure. But we have a situation, Charlie, and I am not sure I know what to do about it. We need to talk about it. It affects us both and I am not sure how to handle it."

"That sounds serious Steve. What is going on?"

"Well, it's Loraine and Claire, they have taken over."

"Taken over what?" Charlie asked.

"They have taken over the business," replied Steve.

"I see. So let me guess. Loraine has started to work some, and she is taking over. And Claire is involved now and between the two of them they are finding all sorts of new ways to do things. They are coming up with new ideas and making plans and you are no longer in control. As a matter of fact, if you're not careful you will be working for them. Am I right?'

"Yes, that is it exactly. How did you know?" replied Steve, as if he was surprised Charlie knew this would happen.

"I told you Loraine was a perfectionist when you said you wanted to offer her a job. That she would come in here and work herself to death and you too if she took the job. Remember?"

"Well, yes. I remember. But I didn't think she would have Claire in here too? What am I supposed to do about that?" asked Steve with exasperation in his tone.

"Didn't you know Claire would be coming over now that Loraine was working here?" asked Charlie. "They do everything together. What is Claire wanting to do while she is here at the warehouse?"

"It started out with Loraine contacting the Food Chain and pitching the idea of us creating a new product line of frozen popsicles. Bubba's Frozen treats for kids," said Steve. "You know like the frozen chilly willies we eat around here in the summertime in a plastic wrapper. Taking our lemonade, mango, cherry, and strawberry mix and putting it in plastic wrappers like a freeze pop and selling them in stores. The Food Chain loved the idea and so we are going to be making those and selling them to the Food Chain. Which is a great idea."

"Okay, so how is that a problem?" asked Charlie.

"Well," Steve says, "once Loraine sold the Food Chain on the popsicles idea she talked to Claire and Claire is going to do the artwork for the packaging with a new design of Bubba and you on the package to appeal to kids and hopefully sell in the ballparks around the country now

173

that you are playing in the majors again. Which of course is a great idea."

"Okay, so what is the problem?" Charlie asked again. Knowing full well that the women running Steve out of the building he built, changing his daily routine and taking over the offices and the warehouse, was the real problem.

"The problem is that now Claire is involved in the business, she wants an office down here at the warehouse. She wants to start coming here and working with Loraine on other marketing projects. She wants to become more involved in the business on a day-to-day basis. So, now I will be with her at home, and be with her at work. Not just her, but her and Loraine. They are taking over and before long I will not have a job. They will run me out of here."

"I see," Charlie said, trying not to laugh out loud at Steve's dilemma.

About that time there was a knock on Steve's office door. Jack Reynolds, Steve's father-in-law had dropped by hoping to catch up with Charlie.

"Hey, there Charlie Pace," Jack said as he walked in the office door and gave Charlie a firm handshake, then taking a seat next to Charlie across from Steve's desk. "We sure are proud of you Charlie. It's been a real treat watching you pitch this summer. Seeing you on national television. Congratulations on making the playoffs and clinching the division. I hope you guys win the whole thing this year."

"Thanks Jack, it has been a great season," Charlie replied as he sat back down in his chair. "Look Jack, I am glad you have come by, we have a situation here at the lemonade company and you are just the man to advise me and Steve what to do."

"Oh, yeah," said Jack, "what's going on fellas?"

"Loraine has come to work in the business and she is so efficient she has taken over," said Charlie. "Now she and

Claire are both wanting an office here and Steve will soon be out of a job. I'm going to be playing baseball for at least five more years so he will have to be here with the two of them alone. We have already figured out that either of the two women are smarter, more creative, and harder workers than the two of us put together. No way around it. Soon they will figure that out and Steve will be working for the two of them 24/7, and he's not sure what to do about it?"

"I see. Well, there is only one thing to do," said Jack resolutely.

"What's that Jack?" Steve asked.

"You need to semi-retire and not tell anybody," Jack replied.

"How's that?" said Steve.

"Well, you can't outthink these two girls," Jack responded. "They are smarter than we are, and you can't fight it, and once they realize that you are doomed. So, just let them take over. You come and go and keep yourself busy, so you are not here as much. Hire you another person, a man to even out the playing field a bit. Call him your executive assistant. Somebody who has an accounting background that can give you a daily report on inventory, expenses, sales, etc. That way you can keep an eye on things without having to be here all the time. Then you stay out of the office playing golf with customers, doing charity work and volunteering. Call it public relations work and let the girls run the place. They will do a better job than you two guys will anyway and as long as they are in control, they will be happy. Unless they want to do something that is just real, and I mean real crazy, leave them alone. When they ask your opinion about what they want to do, they aren't really asking your opinion. They are telling you what they are going to do anyway. So, unless it is real, real crazy, just agree with them and they will work it out. Remember what I told you when you first got married

Steve. When it comes to relationships with women, you can be right – or you can be happy – but you can't be both. Make it easy on yourself, choose happy."

32

Later that same day, a little after 1, Charlie drove his Jeep into the Myrtle Beach Racquet Club where Loraine and Claire were playing a tennis match with two ladies from their Bible study group. Charlie parked his Jeep in the parking lot to watch the last few points of the match under a shade tree near the clubhouse. Soon after his arrival some teenage kids waiting for the court to open recognized Charlie and asked for his autograph and a photo. Before long the news of Charlie's arrival spread across the clubhouse and people began walking in Charlie's direction congratulating him on his return to Chicago and the team winning the division championship.

By the time Loraine and Claire's tennis match ended, Charlie was surrounded by adoring fans. Loraine and Claire made their way over to where Charlie was standing signing autographs and posing for pictures.

"I think Charlie likes all this attention more than he lets on," Loraine said laughingly as she and Claire walked toward Charlie and the crowd of people standing around him.

"I don't know about that," responded Claire. "Charlie has done everything he could to avoid being in the limelight since I met him six years ago. He might not like it as much as you think. But Charlie can't say no when someone asks him for something. He is generous to a fault sometimes. Haven't you noticed that about him, Loraine?"

"Yes, you're right. I was only joking about that. Charlie will bend over backwards for someone whenever he is asked to do something. I could tell that the first time I saw him at a Bubba Ball event this past spring. He stayed out on the field for an hour or so after the event ended talking to parents and the kids who came that day. I know he gets tired of people coming up to him and asking for an autograph. But I have never seen him walk away from a kid who asked him for an autograph or a photo."

For the next 30 minutes or so Loraine hung around as Charlie obliged the crowd of fans waiting to meet him and shake his hand. Then once the crowd thinned out the two of them hopped into Charlie's Jeep with Bubba lying on the floorboard behind them and drove to a local restaurant to grab some lunch. After lunch they drove to Loraine's apartment where they changed into bathing suits and headed out onto the beach where they lounged around the rest of the afternoon.

Once they got out onto the beach Charlie put on some suntan lotion and lying beneath a large beach umbrella, he quickly drifted off to sleep. It had been a busy ten weeks for Charlie since leaving for Chicago. This day, being alone with Loraine, on a quiet weekday afternoon at the beach was just the therapy Charlie needed for his sore body. Charlie had pitched more innings this summer baseball season than he had pitched during the two previous years combined. His body and his mind needed a break as he and the team prepared to make a playoff run.

For Loraine, the summer had been a dream. One unexpected turn of events after another had come her way. And she was almost immediately moved to tears, as she sat there in a beach chair thinking about all the unplanned blessings she had received over the past months since moving to Myrtle Beach for the summer. Lying next to a man she had met just five months ago; Loraine's life had somehow fallen into place. For the first time in many, many years, maybe for the first time in her life, she felt at peace. She had found home.

It was a warm breezy afternoon. The wind coming from the east off the ocean, blowing her hair gently behind her. The suntan lotion covering her lean athletic body, the sun gently caressing her soft supple skin. It seemed too good to be true. She reached out and held Charlie's hand as he laid there quietly sleeping beside her. She wondered if she and Charlie would soon have children of their own playing in the surf? Would they one day be watching their children playing in the sand from beach chairs, just like these? Charlie resting quietly beside her, children of their own playing beside them. It seemed like a dream.

Over the past weeks since the marriage proposal, Loraine began to believe good things could happen for her. From her childhood, when she was only seven years old, the year her father and mother divorced, Loraine had battled feelings of insecurity. Although she seldom spoke of it, Loraine understood what it was like to feel rejected. To feel unwanted. The fact was, Loraine rarely saw her father from the day he left her and her mother to fend for themselves 24 summers ago.

The feeling of insecurity caused by her parents' divorce, left Loraine shaken and unsettled emotionally. Her stunning beauty and her keen mind covered up the scars of a confused and fragile child. Her work ethic, drove her to prove herself. If she could only be good enough. If she could only work hard enough. If she could only be athletic enough, or pretty enough, or try hard enough. She would never be left behind again.

She had been reluctant to go out with Charlie when he first asked her out, one because it could affect her job, and her job, her sense of accomplishment and proving herself gave her a sense of self-worth. A feeling that she could make it on her own no matter what. But also, Loraine didn't trust men. Not just Charlie, any man. She had seen the heartache of being an only child, living with her mother who battled her own feelings of insecurity after the man she loved walked out on her and left her to raise a child on her own.

So, as Loraine sat there beside a man who loved her, the tears began to flow. Charlie was a good man with a big heart and a kind and gentle nature. A man she could trust. Someone who she could depend on. While Charlie lay there quietly sleeping beside her, Loraine began to let the pain go. Little by little, the tears became a river of emotion. Not tears of sadness, tears of joy. Loraine knew she was home. Loraine knew she had met people who cared about her and loved her unconditionally. Charlie and his family. Claire, Doris, Steve and Jack. Steve and Claire's children. Her new friends from working at the ballpark and now in the Lemonade Company. People she had met in her new church, her Bible study group. Somehow, when she least expected it, Loraine was home.

As she sat their trying to compose herself and not wake Charlie, Loraine began to pray.

"Lord, I can't believe how you brought me here today. I never would have dreamed these wonderful things would have happened to me. I am sorry Lord, that for a long time I did not believe. I did not believe in good things. I lost my faith in your goodness. I guess my heart was so broken only You could mend it.

"I thank you Lord for Charlie. I thank you for my new friends and the people here who have been so, so good to me. People whom I did not know and only met just a short time ago. Please Father, help me to be the wife, and prayerfully the mother, you would have me to be one day. Please watch over us, and I ask that you bless Charlie and me with children of our own one day. I ask this in the name

of your Son, Jesus. I now believe, through Him all things are possible. In Jesus name I pray, Amen."

Then, with the gentle breeze blowing against her tanned skin, Loraine laid her head back against the chair and drifted off to sleep.

She was home.

33

It was just past 8:30 the following morning when Charlie placed Bubba's food bowl on the tile floor in his kitchen. In less than a minute Bubba had cleaned out his bowl. Then he slopped up some water from his water bowl, and soon was looking up in Charlie's direction and barking a couple of times to signal he was ready to go outside. By 8:45 Charlie had slipped on his wet suit and some water shoes, and he and Bubba were headed out the door across the wood decking and down to the pier where Charlie's kayak was waiting.

It was a cool September morning, a light haze over the intercoastal waterway, as Charlie lifted the kayak from its position on the pier and placed it in the water. There were a few minutes of light stretching, then Charlie and Bubba took their places in the kayak and began their journey across the waterway and out into the sound, leading toward the ocean.

A calm morning with hardly any breeze, the water was still, almost like a lake as Charlie and Bubba made their way out into the ocean and headed south down the shoreline. Charlie was still experiencing some soreness in his right shoulder and elbow, so he took it easy as he paddled the kayak along the shoreline. For the next 30 minutes or so the two of them headed south about 50 yards from the beach. Then once they reached the Apache Pier, Charlie steered the kayak toward land. He pulled the kayak on the beach as Bubba jumped into the water before walking ashore. Charlie spent the next 20 minutes doing some more stretching and ran a few wind sprints along the ocean's edge. Then once the running was complete Charlie and Bubba made the 100 yard or so walk up the sand dunes to the convenient store beside the pier.

"Hey there Mr. Jones," Charlie said as he and Bubba entered the convenient store. "How have you been doing? Haven't seen you in a while."

"Hey there Charlie. Good to see you, Buddy!" Mr. Jones said as he reached out and shook Charlie's hand, then bending over and rubbing Bubba's head. "It is good to see y'all. I have missed seeing you two guys!"

"Hey, we have missed seeing you too Mr. Jones. You been behaving yourself since we've seen you last?" Charlie asked as he gave Mr. Jones a hug.

"Yeah, yeah, I have to behave now. Old guys like me, we don't have many chances to misbehave when you get to be my age. Hey Charlie, I have been watching you pitch on the television. You have done great. I tell my wife every time you come on the TV that I know you. She doesn't care a thing about sports, but every time you come on the TV, she watches you the entire game. And if you come out of the game, she quits watching and leaves the room to go watch her reality TV shows. I think she is one of your biggest fans. She will be so excited when she hears you came by the store this morning. We are so proud of you Charlie."

"Hey thanks Mr. Jones. Be sure and tell your wife I appreciate her support. Mr. Jones, I think me, and Bubba will have three, make that four sausage and egg biscuits and a bottle of water for Bubba and an orange juice for me."

For the next 30 minutes Charlie and Bubba hung out in the store with Mr. Jones as they ate their food and caught up on all that was going on in each other's lives. Mr. Jones was about the same age as Charlie's father Ed. Being around Mr. Jones gave Charlie a sense of normalcy. In the quiet convenient store with very few people around, Charlie was able to step away from the limelight a bit. There standing beside his dog, dripping with water in a wet suit, the customers coming in and out of the store did not recognize him. As more people came in and out of the store, no one asking for an autograph, not having to pose for pictures, Charlie became more and more at ease.

The soreness in his shoulder and elbow now was becoming more persistent. Nothing like before when he needed surgery on his right elbow, no sharp pain. No numbness in his arm or fingers, just the aches and pain from a long baseball season that was nearing its conclusion. Still, the pain was there. It was manageable for now, but where the weeks had worn on, the soreness had become a consistent daily reminder that his arm was getting tired. Charlie wondered how many good innings he had left in his right arm this season before having to shut it down for an extended rest.

Later that day Charlie and Bubba dropped by the lemonade company where they met Loraine, Steve and Claire. Loraine showed Charlie her new office, which just so happened to be Charlie's old office. Then she and Claire showed Charlie the plans for remodeling the warehouse to accommodate Claire's new office and a much smaller office Charlie would be using whenever he was back in town and wanted to stop by. They even had a place for Bubba in Charlie's new office. Not as big or spacious as Bubba had before but manageable. And Loraine said whenever Bubba was at the warehouse, he could stay in the office with her, Charlie's old office if he liked.

Loraine and Claire told Charlie about the new packaging design for the Frozen Popsicle product they would be making. Everyone agreed that it was a brilliant idea to use their same product mix and repackage it to create a completely new product line with minimal expense. This new idea of Loraine's and the packaging design by Claire, would be a great asset for the company. Steve and Charlie knew that the two girls could run the place without them no question about it. So, they embraced the ladies' ideas, and the girls were thrilled to be more involved in the success of the family business.

As Loraine and Claire were telling Charlie their plans, he and Steve stood there quietly. Not saying anything other than, "This sounds great. Oh, that will be perfect." Remembering Jack's words of advice, "You can be right – or you can be happy - but you can't be both." Charlie and Steve wisely chose happy.

This would be Charlie's last night in Myrtle Beach before heading back to Chicago for the last series of the regular season. The team had decided that since the division was clinched Charlie would not pitch in this series. Instead, he and the other starters would rest their arms this weekend to be ready for the first round of the playoffs the following Friday night in Chicago against eastern division champion Detroit.

It was later that evening, just after six when Charlie arrived at Loraine's condo to pick her up for dinner. The two of them drove north up Hwy 17 to the Dunes Club. When they entered the room every head in the building turned in their direction. Many people recognizing Charlie, but everyone noticed Loraine. She was as beautiful that night as she had ever been. Wearing a short tight fitting yellow dress. Not the kind of dress any woman could wear. Loraine was stunning. Her tanned skin. Her long slender legs. The tightly fitting dress accentuating the cures in her athletic, lean body. She was gorgeous. Even Charlie's celebrity status could not overshadow Loraine's natural beauty.

Once they reached their table, they ordered dinner and a bottle of wine. After dinner they went out onto the balcony overlooking the ocean.

"Loraine, you are always beautiful, but I have never seen you more beautiful than tonight," Charlie said as he reached out and took Loraine by the hand.

"Thank you, Charlie. I don't think I have ever been as happy as I am now, and I owe that to you. I love you, Charlie. You have been so good to me. Because of you, I have met so many people who have been so good to me since moving here this summer. I never would have expected all this and I love my new job. My life is in such a good place now. I am so, so happy.

"I'm glad you like your job, and the popsicle idea," Charlie declared, "what a great idea. And Claire seems to be happy to be more involved in the business. That's great that you both will be able to work together on these ideas. I am sure you two will come up with many other ways to make the business better."

"Charlie, I do have a question about the business," said Loraine.

Immediately Charlie felt a lump in his throat. *"Oh my gosh, here it comes, why didn't I tell her I owned the business."*

"Sure, what's that Loraine?" Charlie said as calmly as he could under the circumstances.

"Why didn't you tell me earlier you and Steve co-owned the lemonade company?" asked Loraine as she squeezed Charlie's hand just enough to get his attention. Looking in his direction, "didn't you think I would find out sooner or later?"

"Think, think, think, think, think" flashed through Charlie's mind as he smiled back in Loraine's direction. He was busted and he knew it. She knew, she had known for

some time now. He had not told her. He was in trouble and there was no escaping this. What would he say? He smiled a little longer trying to think of something to say. But he had nothing.

"I have known you and Steve owned the lemonade company from the first week I got here. Doris told me. Everyone at the stadium, the vendors, the folks working in the concession stand, the ladies in our Bible study know you and Steve own the business together. So, why didn't you tell me?" Loraine asked again.

Then it hit Charlie, exactly what to say.

"Well Loraine, I just assumed you knew. Like you were saying, Doris knows, the vendors know, the folks working in the concession stands know, the ladies in your Bible Study know. I don't try to hide it. I just never talk about it much because Steve does all the work down there and I wanted him to get the credit for the company's success. I just assumed you knew."

Loraine looked intently at Charlie. He smiled as much as he could and tried to remain calm. He had thrown this out there and he was sticking with it. Loraine knew she had caught him, but she couldn't prove that he was playing the assume card. So, she made him squirm a little more before letting Charlie off the hook.

"So, you just assumed I knew. And that's why you didn't tell me," Loraine said as she looked intently into Charlie's eyes and squeezed his hand a little tighter. Letting him know she did not believe his excuse for a second.

"Ouch Loraine, that's a strong grip. And that's my pitching hand you are strangling there."

"You assumed," Loraine said squeezing Charlie's hand a little tighter.

"Maybe," Charlie said.

"Well, just so we get this straight, if we have anything else you are involved in you are going to tell me about it before I hear it from someone else. Correct?"

"Yes, ma'am. I will."

34

Friday afternoon about 4:30 Charlie arrived at Belmont Park. He went into the players locker room where he was greeted by team managers on his way to the trainer's room. There he was given a massage to loosen up his aching body before taking the field for warm-ups. With the soreness in his shoulder persisting, even after having a two-week rest between tonight and his last start in St. Louis, Charlie understood that this pain in his right arm would not go away until the season was over and he rested his arm several weeks. Charlie had pitched in the big leagues for an entire season three times before earlier in his career. He and the training staff understood that in professional baseball, there are only so many innings per year in a pitcher's arm. So, with the support of management, the coaching staff and trainers, Chicago was trying to get as many quality innings out of Charlie's right arm as they could before the end of the season.

After his therapy massage Charlie joined the rest of his teammates in the locker room. Even though tonight marked the first playoff appearance for Chicago in over 15 seasons, the mood was light and upbeat in the Chicago clubhouse before the game. Chicago was a heavy favorite to beat their opponents from Detroit. Tonight's game would be the first in a seven-game series with the first two games being played in Chicago, followed by three in Detroit and then two more games in Chicago if necessary. Chicago had an 8-2 record over Detroit in the regular season in head-to-head games. At the end of the regular season, Chicago had the second most wins in professional baseball, trailing only the defending world champion Nashville Knights.

The stadium was nearly full by 6:05 as Charlie exited the locker room and walked onto the field. Game time for tonight's contest was at 7:05. With the Chicago crowd at a fever pitch even an hour before the game was scheduled to begin, Charlie calmly walked out of the dugout and down the right field line toward the bullpen for his pregame warm up. Fans standing on their feet clapping and shouting their support for Charlie as he made his way through the outfield.

At 6:50 both teams stood along their respective baselines for the playing of the National Anthem. Then at 7:00 sharp with Loraine, Steve, Claire, and Charlie's family all watching from the players box behind the Chicago first base dugout, Charlie walked out of the Chicago dugout toward the mound as the rest of the Chicago starting line-up ran out of the dugout to their positions in the field. As the team raced onto the field, the Belmont Park fans stood to their feet and a roar echoed throughout the stadium. With 15 seasons of missing the playoffs finally coming to an end, the Chicago fans were filled with pent up energy as the long-suffering frustration of missing the playoffs was finally over.

It was 7:05 when Charlie stood behind the mound. Alone with the baseball in his hand, he calmly walked to the top of the mound and toed the pitching rubber, looking in for the catcher's signal. He nodded his head in acknowledgement of the sign. He looked above the brim of the baseball glove covering his left hand. Peering in toward his target he started his windup and delivered the game's first pitch. 101 MPH flashed on the radar gun on top of the centerfield scoreboard. Strike one.

For the next two hours Charlie was in complete control of the Detroit hitters. Striking out 14 Detroit batters over seven innings as Chicago took a commanding 6-0 lead before Charlie was relieved in the top of the eighth. With Romero coming into the game in relief and pitching two solid innings, Chicago cruised to a 7-2 victory.

Chicago would go on to win games two and three, to take a 3-0 lead in the series before losing the fourth game to Detroit, 4-3, forcing a game five in Detroit. In game five Charlie was again scheduled to pitch and on that cool windy night in Detroit, Charlie once more went seven strong innings before being relieved by Romero in the eighth. Chicago would go on to win game five by a score of 3-2, setting up a meeting with the defending World Champion Nashville Knights.

After the deciding game five, Charlie spoke with the press in the Detroit media center.

"Charlie, congratulations on the win tonight. How are you feeling about the team's chances against the defending World Champion Nashville Knights?" asked a reporter from one of the national sports networks.

"Nashville has a super baseball team. We split our head-to-head games with them 5-5 during the regular season, so we have a lot of respect for those guys. They have a great hitting team and pitching staff. It will be a challenge for sure. But we have been playing solid baseball all season as well. It should be a great series."

"How is your arm feeling Charlie?" asked a reporter from the Sports Channel.

"I'm tired," Charlie said with exasperation, causing a sympathetic laugh of agreement among the crowd in the press core. "But hey, that's part of baseball. After a 162-game regular season and now playing in the playoffs, everyone on the roster is banged up some and tired. My arm feels fine all things considered. I am excited for my next opportunity to pitch, and I will be ready when they pencil me in the lineup."

35

The following Tuesday morning Charlie and Steve walked into the Chicago baseball organization offices at Belmont Park on their way to their 11 am meeting with Herb Volkmann. Once they reached Herb's office, he was still tied up in an earlier meeting, so the two men took a seat in the reception area. It was 11:15 before Herb's prior meeting concluded and he came out into the reception area to greet Steve and Charlie.

"Good morning fellas. It's good to see you guys this morning, come on in and have a seat," said Herb as walked out of his office and warmly shook the two men's hands.

"Thanks Herb," Steve replied. "We appreciate you taking the time out of your busy schedule for us to come up and meet with you."

"You're welcome, guys," Herb said as he sat down behind his desk. Charlie and Steve now sitting in the leather chairs across from Herb. "I am excited to hear more about what we discussed over the phone the other day. Oftentimes in my job, my meetings are about someone wanting this or needing that or how much money we are going to spend on this contract or the other. It's not everyday I get to discuss a project that is good for the community and can help us reach kids in need without someone asking me to only gift them money. We want to be more involved in the community, but we only have so many resources and we can't help everyone. I am really excited about your proposal, and I have discussed it preliminarily with management and they seem very interested in learning more about what you guys are wanting to do."

"Well, that's great Herb," said Charlie. "This was Steve's idea, so I want to let him tell you about it."

"Great," said Herb. "Go ahead Steve, tell me more about what you are proposing to do here in Chicago and how we might be a part of this youth program."

"Herb, I know you are familiar with our Bubba Ball program we sponsor through the lemonade company. You have been kind enough to allow us to use the Seahawk Stadium in Myrtle Beach for several years now to host the events. We appreciate the Seahawks willingness to support us.

"And like you and I have discussed in the past, disadvantaged and trouble youth, particularly the children in the foster care system have a special place in my heart, since I grew up in the foster care system myself. We have been so blessed, Charlie and I, through the success of the lemonade company, we want to give back. To share some of the blessings we have received.

"You know that we sponsor baseball clinics in Seahawk's stadium from March through September once a month. Bubba's Ball baseball camp is free of charge to any child in our area who would like to attend. We also hold a Bubba Ball clinic in the afternoon those same days for children with special needs and their families. We provide lunch along with a hat and t-shirt to every kid who attends. This in turn creates an opportunity for the Seahawk players to help, sign autographs and give instructions to the kids and meet the parents. The events have been a huge success. We also sponsor a traveling 16-under AAU team with an emphasis on providing the funding and coaching for kids whose families otherwise may not be able to afford for their child to participate in more competitive travel baseball training. And our 16-under AAU team is one of the top ranked teams in the southeastern United States. So, needless to say we are very proud of this Bubba Ball Program."

"You should be," Herb replied. "I think this is great. I love everything about it. Tell me how we could help with this?"

"We would like to expand our outreach with the Bubba Ball program Herb, like we talked about the other day over the phone. We want to hold an event here in Chicago next spring to kick that off here at Belmont Park," said Charlie. "I have spoken with some of the other players on the team here and they would like to help with this. Some want to donate money, and others want to help run the clinics. We have had very good support from the players. Some of the guys on the roster here in Chicago helped with the Bubba Ball clinics in Myrtle Beach when they were playing ball there in the minor leagues, so they are familiar with how this works and want to help here in Chicago as well."

"I think it is a great idea," said Herb. "And I can tell you management has agreed to let you use Belmont Park next spring to hold the events. We would also by willing to help donate some money to the program and be a co-sponsor as well."

36

"Ladies and gentlemen, this is Bill Thomas, along with my partner Greg Wilson, on Chicago's own, WCGN Radio. Coming to you live tonight with our Chicago Baseball Team Official pre-game show, from historic Volunteer Stadium, in Nashville Tennessee. Home of the defending World Champion Nashville Knights for the seventh game of our seven game League Championship series. With a ticket to the World Championship Series going to the winner of tonight's ball game scheduled to begin at 7:05 pm central time.

"Just to give you a quick recap of how we got here tonight. The Knights won the first two games of the series played here in Nashville. Then in Chicago, behind the stellar pitching of Charlie Pace we won game three. The Chicago team would go on to win the next two games of the series in Chicago to take a 3-2 series lead. Then last night here in Nashville, the Knights won a thrilling 12 inning game in Volunteer Stadium to even the series at three games apiece, setting the stage for tonight's deciding seventh game. There has been some sensational baseball played in this championship series with three of the sixth games going into extra innings.

"We expect another exciting game tonight when Chicago right hander Charlie Pace will be putting his perfect 14-0 record on the line as he seeks to pitch Chicago to the World Championship Series for the first time in 32 years. Meanwhile, Nashville will be pitching their all-star left hander, Jerry Thomas, as he attempts to pitch Nashville back to the World Championship Series for the third consecutive season. Thomas with a major league leading record of 23 wins against only three losses on the season."

"It has been a magical season for Chicago baseball fans, Bill" says Greg Thomas the other WCGN announcer. "We knew before the season began that Chicago would be a playoff contender this season. These past few years management has developed some fine young players in our farm system, and the veterans returning this season gave us all high hopes that this year we might get back into the playoffs. But it has been the pitching of former Most Outstanding Player Award Winner Charlie Pace that has in my opinion put Chicago over the top, from being a competitive team to becoming a bonified championship contender. Tonight, with a trip to the World Championship of professional baseball on the line, Chicago will turn to Pace one more time to see if he can take us all the way to the World Championship Series."

Leading off the top of the first inning for Chicago was centerfielder Mike Lyndon. With the count two balls and one strike Lyndon hit a belt high fastball thrown by Nashville pitcher Jerry Thomas deep into the left field bleachers for a homerun, giving Chicago an early 1-0 lead. Then for the next eight innings Thomas and Charlie Pace were locked in a classic pitching duel. With Chicago taking a 1-0 lead through the bottom of the eighth inning. With Charlie throwing 125 pitches through the eighth, allowing no runs on only six hits but giving up four walks. When Charlie reached the dugout steps after pitching his way out of a bases loaded jam in the bottom of the eighth, he was met by Chicago manager, Ed Finch.

"Charlie, you have pitched a great ballgame tonight. How are you feeling? Do you think you can go back out there in the ninth and finish the game or do we need to go to the bullpen? How is your arm?" asked coach Finch.

"I don't think I have another good inning left in me tonight, Coach," Charlie replied. "I think we need to bring in a reliever to pitch the ninth."

So, in the bottom of the ninth rookie reliever Juan Romero came into pitch. The first Knight's batter fouled off six two strike pitches before working Romero for a walk. Then on the very next pitch, Nashville Allstar third baseman Steve Stutts, hit a Romero curve ball 450 feet over the center field fence. Giving the Knights a 2-1 victory and ending the Chicago team's season.

As Romero reached the Chicago dugout Charlie was standing on the top of the dugout steps to meet him. Placing his arm around Romero, Charlie walked his friend and protégé into the dugout where they sat quietly side by side watching the Knights players and fans celebrate their victory.

After the game Charlie spoke with the press in the Knights media center.

"Charlie, another great performance tonight," stated a reporter from a local sports channel. "Tough way to end the season."

"Yes, that was a tough loss tonight. Great game. Great series," said Charlie. "There really are no losers in a game or a series like this. But it sure hurts to be on the losing end of a game like tonight. It will sting for a while that's for sure. But we had a great season and there is no reason for anyone to hang their heads about tonight's game."

"What about Romero," asked a syndicated sportswriter from Chicago. "He has had a great rookie season. How will a loss like tonight affect a young pitcher like Romero?"

"Romero has pitched well for us all season. We would not have made it this far if it were not for his contribution as a starter and pitching in relief. Romero is a tough, resilient kid. He has a bright future ahead of him.

"We have some talented young players on this team and a nucleus of solid returning players. This was a tough loss tonight, but we will be back ready to go in the spring. And I think if this team stays healthy, we have the ability to be competing for a World Championship again next year, no doubt about it."

37

"Are you nervous?" Steve asked Charlie as the two of them stood alone inside the church parlor Steve adjusting Charlie's bowtie.

"Yeah, a little bit. It's not every day you get married. But I know Loraine is the one for me. I am so happy; I can't be too nervous," Charlie replied.

"Well, that's a good way to look at it I'd say. I don't think you could have ever found a better fit for you Charlie. That Loraine, she is tough. She is not going to put up with a whole lot of mess from you. I can see that after working with her for a few weeks now. She is going to keep you straight."

"Yeah, I know," agreed Charlie. "There is not going to be any hiding things from Loraine. I am going to try and give her as much space as I can and not suggest too much. Once she makes up her mind about something she is not very interested in any input from me on whatever it is she is doing. So, I am going to try not to be disagreeing with her any more than I can help.

"You know I have been thinking a lot about what Jack told us, about having a long-lasting marriage. You can be right, or you can be happy – but you can't be both. I think he is 100% right about that. I talked to my dad about it, and he told me basically the same thing, happy wife, happy life. There are many, many things Loraine cares very strongly about that don't mean a thing to me. So, I am going to take their advice and try and stay out of those things as much as I can and let her do what she wants, as long as it doesn't affect me too much.

"I think we will get along a lot better if I let her make those decisions and spend my time doing the things I want to do and leave the rest to her."

"She is smarter than you are anyway," said Steve chuckling. "It's the same at my house. Claire can do most anything better than me and she likes being in control. When I go along and try and do what she suggests, most of the time things work out better anyway.

"I thought it was really neat that your dad is going to walk Loraine down the aisle today, Charlie," said Steve.

"Yeah, me to. Loraine and her father have not had any sort of a relationship for over 20 years now, and dad, he loves Loraine. Not having a daughter of his own he has always tried to be very conscious of my brothers' wives. It meant a lot to him when she agreed to let him be the one to walk her down the aisle. He looks at Loraine as if she were his daughter, I can see that already."

It was about 20 minutes later when the church pastor came into the parlor. After a quick prayer, the pastor, Charlie and Steve entered the church sanctuary and took their places standing near the front of the church. Soon the procession of the mothers and the wedding party began. Then, when the doors opened and Loraine and Ed appeared in the hallway beyond the church sanctuary entrance, Charlie was nearly overcome with emotion. As Loraine and his father began to walk slowly toward him, in that moment, it was as if Charlie's past flashed before him. The pain and heartache of his injury to his arm and his first divorce. The loneliness of his rehabilitation and the depression and addiction that followed. The nights he spent alone in his condo as he battled his demons, hoping and praying that he could regain his confidence and put his health and life back together. All those painful memories seemed to go before him and passed beyond him as he watched his father, the man he admired most in the world, walking the love of his life down the aisle until they took their places next to him.

"Who gives this woman to be married to this man?" asked the pastor.

"Loraine's mother and I," said Charlie's father as he lifted Loraine's vale. Then kissing her on the cheek, he turned and sat down next to Charlie's mother.

Loraine was lovely in her wedding dress, as she stood there beside Charlie with trembling knees. Being married was not something she had in her plans a few months ago. Taking a leap of faith with a man she had only known for a few months was not the type of thing the perfectionist Loraine would have done before moving to the beach. Before the long morning jogs along the shoreline. The laid-back barbecues. The Sunday morning church services and Bible studies with her new friends. The day trips to the beach with Claire and the kids. Shopping with Doris and her daughters and the ladies she worked with at the ballpark.

No, Loraine was a different person now. Her father-in-law, who adored her like the daughter he never had, now sitting behind her. Friends and family gathered around. Loraine and Charlie stood their side-by-side, the way newlyweds do. Not knowing what the future holds, committing to face what would come their way together. They took their vows and pledged to love one another until death do us part, in sickness and in health, for better or worse. Before God and witnesses they made this commitment to each another.

Later after the wedding there was a reception at the marina where they went on their first date. A band played local beach music and friends and family from Myrtle Beach and Chicago attended the event. They had their first dance as a newlywed couple, and both Charlie's father, Ed, and

Herb Volkmann, danced a father daughter dance with Loraine. Each man standing in to publicly acknowledge their love and affection for her.

Once the bouquet of flowers had been tossed and the reception ended, the bride and groom went back to Loraine's condo to spend their first night together before heading off on a two-week honeymoon to St. Thomas.

Later that night about 3:30 in the morning, Charlie got up from their bed and walked out onto the balcony of Loraine's condo as she lay sleeping. He quietly opened the balcony door and took a seat in one of the chairs looking out toward the ocean. The moonlight shimmering formed a straight line across the ocean waters in his direction. The waves moving on shore one after another in a rhythmic motion, the sound of the water crashing upon the shore, a stiff breeze blowing off the ocean from the southeast. Charlie sat there thinking about all that had happened to him these past few months. It seemed like a dream. It seemed too good to be true. It seemed like a miracle. It was a miracle.

Quietly, alone in the moonlight, the superstar baseball player wiped a tear from his eye. Then another. Then another. Tears of happiness. Tears of relief. Tears of thankfulness. Charlie's life, his recovery, his return to health. They were miracles, and Charlie knew it. He knew where the miracles we call blessings come from. He bowed his head in the darkness and prayed.

"Lord, I am thankful for my family who love me. I am thankful for my new wife, Loraine. What a blessing she is to me. I am thankful to have my health back. To have my mind back, my confidence back. I am thankful for Steve and his family and what they have done for me. I am thankful for Herb Volkmann, my teammates and our coaches. I am thankful for our business and all the people who are involved with that.

"Lord, you have blessed me abundantly, and I want to give back from all you have given me so that other people may come to know you more intimately. Lord, you have given me so much, and there is so much need in the world, it is overwhelming to think of all the people who would benefit by knowing you. Lord, I will go wherever you want me to go, and I will do whatever you want me to do, to help reach those people. I pray Lord, that you would open the right doors, at just the right time, to use me to help teach others about you. That I would be able to be a witness for you. To thank you for all you have done for me. Thank you again for everything Lord. In Jesus name I pray, Amen."

38

On a breezy Sunday evening a month later, Charlie Pace walked across a temporary stage placed across the infield in Seahawk Stadium. There before a crowd of 5000 plus spectators he took a seat behind the on-stage podium. After a few hymns sung by a local choir and an introduction from his church pastor, Charlie walked calmly toward the podium.

"I would like to thank you all for coming out tonight, and I would like to thank everyone who has contributed to the planning and organization of tonight's event. We hope that it will be a blessing to everyone who is here tonight.

"I would like to begin tonight by reading a passage from the Gospel of Luke, Chapter 10.

"One day an expert in religious law stood up to test Jesus by asking him this question: "Teacher, what should I do to inherit eternal life?"

"Jesus replied, "What does the law of Moses say? How do you read it?"

"The man answered, 'You must love the Lord your God with all your heart, all your soul, all your strength, and all your mind.' And, 'Love your neighbor as yourself.'

"Right!" Jesus told him. "Do this and you will live!"

"The man wanted to justify his actions, so he asked Jesus, "And who is my neighbor?"

"Jesus replied with a story: '"A Jewish man was traveling from Jerusalem down to Jericho, and he was attacked by bandits. They stripped him of his clothes, beat him up, and left him half dead beside the road.

"By chance a priest came along. But when he saw the man lying there, he crossed to the other side of the road and passed him by. A Temple assistant walked over and looked at him lying there, but he also passed by on the other side.

"Then a despised Samaritan came along, and when he saw the man, he felt compassion for him. Going over to him, the Samaritan soothed his wounds with olive oil and wine and bandaged them. Then he put the man on his own donkey and took him to an inn, where he took care of him. The next day he handed the innkeeper two silver coins, telling him, 'Take care of this man. If his bill runs higher than this, I'll pay you the next time I'm here.'

"Now which of these three would you say was a neighbor to the man who was attacked by bandits?" Jesus asked.

"The man replied, "'The one who showed him mercy."

"Then Jesus said, "Yes, now go and do the same."

"What must I do to inherit eternal life? That is the question the expert in religious law asks Jesus. What must I do to inherit eternal life? That is the question people are asking today nearly 2000 years later. It is the question of every person's lifetime. The question for all time. A question that every one of us will wrestle with at some point in our lives.

"Ten years ago, I went through a very dark period in my life. I went from having everything I thought I could ever hope for to being alone; injured emotionally and physically in what seemed like overnight. Suddenly, all the things I had placed my hope and trust in were gone. Mentally during all this, I spiraled out of control. Self-confidence was never an issue for me before my injury. I thought I could do anything on my own. I could handle whatever came my way. But when so many things changed overnight and I was in a place where everything that could go wrong did go wrong and I could do nothing to fix it, I became deeply depressed.

"During that point I was taking prescription pain killers for a staph infection in my arm and soon those pain meds became a crutch for me to cope with my emotional pain and my physical pain as well. I have been a Christian all my life. I first accepted Christ at a young age. But I never understood the life of Christ, or what it meant to live out a Christian life until I found myself left on the side of the road, like the man in the story. Then amazingly, somehow, in answer to my prayers for help, God sent these amazing, loving, caring people into my life who came and helped me. They spent time with me. They did not judge me. They invited me to church and to join a Bible study. They walked along side me as God healed me. They did not fix my problems. They could not fix what had happened to me or the choices I made when I was hurting. But they were there. I could feel their presence and that made the difference.

"God used these people to heal me. They were God's hands and feet to do His will and by watching them I learned what it meant to be a follower of Christ.

"Maybe you find yourself like I was tonight. You feel as though you have been left on the side of the road as the world passes you by. Maybe you are struggling with the loss of a job, or the end of a career and you wonder if God or anyone else cares? Maybe you are battling an illness or an addiction? Or maybe you are the caregiver for an elderly parent or a sick child or spouse, and you wonder if God cares? There is something I can tell you tonight for certain. All of us at some point if we live long enough, will experience what it is like to be the man in the story, left alongside the road. I never would have imagined it could have happened to me, but it did. And oddly enough, today I thank God for that. I thank God that I was left on the side of the road. Because it was there, where I found God.

"You see, when nearly everyone else turned their back on me and left me for dead, that is when I could see God working through these amazing people to rescue me. It was these amazing people who showed up on His behalf and gave me a glimpse into what it was like to share kindness, mercy and compassion. Not because they wanted anything from me, or because I was wealthy, or popular. No, it was because they had studied the life of Jesus and they were His followers living out the message of the Gospel. They simply did what Jesus teaches us to do when we study the four accounts of His ministry found in the Bible.

"You may not think the Gospel message is relevant in our world today. After all, the Bibles most contemporary writings were written nearly 2000 years ago. But I can tell you from my personal experience, that reading and studying the Bible, with the help and support of these people in our small local church, saved me. Reading my Bible and learning more about Jesus Christ and His ministry helped me to find purpose and meaning in my life when all hope seemed lost.

"For someone who does not actively read and study the Bible like a textbook, it could be easy to believe the gospel message is not relative to our daily lives. But nothing could be further from the truth. The Bible is a book written for all time, because the message of the Bible is the written message given to us by God Himself, through the work of the various authors of the Bible books, to show us who God is and His plan for us today.

"In a world of 24/7 nonstop bad news, it is easy, to get caught up in the rush of our day to day lives and not make spending quiet time with Jesus a priority. To focus so much on what we think is important and miss out on the relationships that make life special. Like family, friends and faith.

"We must decide, choose if you will, whether spending time with God is important to us. No one can read the Bible for you. God gives us free will, so each of us will choose to spend time with Him or not. And spending time in the Bible, Gods' Word, is how God designed this fellowship to happen and our relationship with God to grow. We and we alone, must choose if that relationship is important to us.

"I can tell you from personal experience, that my relationship with God is the most important relationship in my life. Because when I was left on the side of the road, it was my relationship with Jesus that saved me.

"I can say now with 100% sincerity, no matter where you are or what you may be facing, with Jesus in your life there is always hope."

ABOUT THE AUTHOR

    Donnie Prince is a self-employed business man and author who lives in his home state of North Carolina. He and his wife, Kathy, have two daughters and three awesome grandchildren. For more information visit his website at play2winlive2serve.com.

Other books written by Donnie Prince:

Play 2 Win Live 2 Serve
The Teacher
An Angel's Journal
Baseball It's More than a Game
Disconnected – The Airius Mission
Why Live For Anyone Other Than Jesus?–Nathan Stiles Story

www.ingramcontent.com/pod-product-compliance
Lightning Source LLC
Chambersburg PA
CBHW060639260626
47161CB00008B/2925